"You're going to be

The world went still. There was just her and Flynn and this wild buzzing in her head that warmed her up and turned her inside and out.

He looked like he wanted to say something more, or perhaps do something more, and her whole body tensed in anticipation of whatever it was. But then his hand dropped and he stepped away and she was left standing there when he turned back to his horse.

"I have to get the bridle."

"Yeah," she heard herself say. "I should get going, too."

But then he stopped and her heart went all wild again.

"You're going to be all right, Amy. You really are. You're smart and good at what you do and your heart is in the right place. As difficult as it might be, you're determined to tough it out. I admire that."

He turned and headed off again and she was left standing there, her eyes warming with unshed tears.

Those were the kindest words anyone had said to her.

Dear Reader,

Sometimes life imitates art, and that was certainly the case with *The Cowboy's Dilemma*. While writing the book I learned I would soon be a first-time grandmother.

I did not take the news well. Ask my daughter.

In my defense, my daughter has two years of college left before earning her bachelor's degree. In my mind this was not a good time for a baby.

It's amazing how your life can change in an instant. We had to reenvision our daughter's future, much the same way my heroine, Amy Jensen, would have to do. That future was scary, but Amy trusts everything will be all right.

It would take a special man to see beyond my heroine's pregnancy to the woman beneath. Flynn Gillian is the eldest brother of five, and he's the one everyone in the family can count on to have a level head. But one look into Amy's tear-filled eyes and his world is turned upside down forever. Fall in love? With a pregnant woman? It would never happen. *Right?*

I adored writing about Amy and Flynn. I hope you enjoy reading their love story, too.

Best,

Pam

HOME *on the* RANCH

THE COWBOY'S DILEMMA

— ⚹ —

PAMELA BRITTON

⬥ HARLEQUIN® HOME ON THE RANCH

Recycling programs
for this product may
not exist in your area.

ISBN-13: 978-1-335-54299-1
ISBN-13: 978-1-335-63398-9 (Direct to Consumer edition)

Home on the Ranch: The Cowboy's Dilemma

Printed in U.S.A.

With more than one million books in print, **Pamela Britton** likes to call herself the best-known author nobody's ever heard of. Of course, that changed thanks to a certain licensing agreement with that little racing organization known as NASCAR.

But before the glitz and glamour of NASCAR, Pamela wrote books that were frequently voted the best of the best by the *Detroit Free Press*, Barnes & Noble—two years in a row—and *RT Book Reviews*. She's won numerous awards, including a National Readers' Choice Award and a nomination for the Romance Writers of America Golden Heart® Award.

When not writing books, Pamela is a reporter for a local newspaper. She's also a columnist for the *American Quarter Horse Journal*.

Books by Pamela Britton

Home on the Ranch: Rodeo Legend
Home on the Ranch: Her Cowboy Hero
Home on the Ranch: The Rancher's Surprise

Harlequin Western Romance

Rodeo Legends: Shane

Cowboys in Uniform

Her Rodeo Hero
His Rodeo Sweetheart
The Ranger's Rodeo Rebel
Her Cowboy Lawman
Winning the Rancher's Heart

Visit the Author Profile page
at Harlequin.com for more titles.

For my future grandson. Nana loves you.

Chapter 1

"Please tell me that isn't what I think that is."

Flynn Gillian spun toward the feminine voice, the eviction notice he'd been holding nearly sliding from his fingertips when he spotted the petite brunette who came up behind him.

"Never mind. I can see by your face that it is," she said. "Which means that a day that couldn't possibly get worse suddenly has."

Amy Jensen. That was who she had to be, although he'd never met his dad's tenant before.

She shook her head a little and he thought she might just walk away—she looked like she was having that kind of day. Instead, she plunked down on the concrete landing that stretched across the front of the one-bedroom farmhouse she rented from his family, then tossed her purse off to one side. The thing tipped over, spilling the contents—breath mints, keys, wallet. She didn't seem to notice or care.

"Great."

That was all she said, but in that one word there lay a wealth of emotions. Frustration. Disappointment. Resignation. Maybe he should just set the paper down and walk away.

Except…

He'd never been proof against a woman in distress. Not his little sister, not his mother—back when she'd been alive—and not this one, apparently.

He slid past her, turned back to face her. She rested her chin in her hands, a single tear sliding down her face, and from nowhere came the urge to wipe it away.

"You can go ahead and leave it." She waved a hand at him. "I know I'm behind. I know I was supposed to make a payment before midnight last night even though, really, who's going to make a payment at 11:59 at night, especially when it's all I can do to keep my eyes open lately, which is why I thought there was something seriously wrong with me. Well, that and the fact that I can't keep anything in my stomach, which is why I went to the doctor today thinking—ohhhhh, I don't know—maybe I had cancer or something. But, SURPRISE, I'm not terminally ill. No. I'm just pregnant and the father of my unborn child is a piece of you-know-what who ran off with his fitness trainer, who, by the way, is the size of a twig. They both moved to another city, which is why I can't afford my rental payments, because that piece of you-know-what who was supposed to pay half told me to go fish, but I mean, really, am I surprised? The lease is in my name. And so, my knight in tarnished armor has fled the castle. So much for fairy tales, right?"

She looked ready to lose it. Her voice had gotten higher and higher with each word, her nose redder and redder, and another tear was falling from her eye. He thought about doing as she asked and just leaving, but something made him sit down next to her instead.

"Have you talked to my dad about any of this?"

She leaned away from him, brown hair swinging around to one shoulder as she met his gaze. "Your dad?"

He tipped his cowboy hat back, scooting sideways to give her a bit more space. "I'm Flynn Gillian. Reese, your landlord, is my dad."

She closed her eyes, turned her face away. "Well, of course you are."

What was that supposed to mean?

"No, I haven't talked to him. I honestly thought I would have the money before today. Mrs. Deborah Donatello owes me a bunch of money for all the work I did on her wedding, but in hindsight, maybe I should have given her until 11:58 p.m. to pay me. That way I could make a payment at 11:59." She sucked in another breath. "Hindsight, right?"

Flynn stared down at the toes of his cowboy boots. "Having a tough go of it, are we?"

He heard her sigh. "You might say that."

There was a speck of dirt on the tip of his boot. He tried to brush it off. "My mom used to say 'this, too, shall pass.'"

"Well—" she sighed "—this won't pass for at least another eight months, and then there's the whole other eighteen years to deal with, but we don't need to get into that."

They sat there in silence and he wondered if he should try to pat her back or something. He hated seeing a woman so upset. When a breeze tugged at the leaves of the nearby oaks, he watched as leaves fell to the ground in a brown-hued blizzard. It was the time of day when the sun had sunk so low on the horizon it painted the whole valley in golds and reds. Holidays were coming soon. It'd be Christmas before he knew it.

"You really don't have to stay." She stared at her hands. "I'll figure this out."

"So, you're going to keep it? The baby?"

She inhaled, tipped her head back as if looking to heaven for guidance. "I don't know. I only just found out today." She shook her head. "I was thinking, I don't know, I'd give him or her up for adoption, but then I thought about my childhood and how messed up it was and that here I was being given a chance to do it all over again, only better, and so now…"

She wasn't sure.

"And the dad? Does he know?"

"He knows." She shrugged. "I told him today. Doesn't care. Said I needed to prove it was his. As if I was the one sleeping around." She wiped at her face. "What an idiot I was to think he was 'the one.' More like the one to avoid."

Her voice sounded muffled. He knew she held back more tears, and even though he didn't know her, it broke his heart.

"You know…" He shouldn't do it, not without checking with his dad first, but to hell with it. "I'm just going to rip this thing up for now."

The sound of him tearing the paper filled the air, and out of the corner of his eye he saw her turn toward him again, mouth open in shock. His dad would probably kill him, he thought, tucking the ripped halves back in his pocket. The rental property was a relatively new addition to Gillian Ranch. His brother Carson had built the place, a single-story home tucked into a tiny valley at the south end of their property, right off the main road. It'd been his brother's first major construction project and an homage to the old farmhouses he loved so much. Amy was their first tenant. His dad had said she'd been great…up until now.

"Look, I'll explain to my dad what's going on. He'll understand. You can catch up on your rent later." He stood up, not at all sure how his dad would feel about the arrangement he'd just made, but oh, well. "I'll tell him to call you."

He started to walk away.

"Wait."

He debated with himself whether to pretend he hadn't heard her but ended up turning back. She wiped at her eyes again, quickly, squaring her shoulders.

"I'm not…" She stood and he realized she was a good deal shorter than he was. Pretty, if one liked the damsel-in-distress type, which he very definitely did not. And yet he couldn't seem to take his eyes off her heart-shaped face.

"I can't take your charity."

Yes, she could, because no matter the brave smile she might try to put on, this was a woman about to face some serious life decisions.

Pregnant. Alone. Broke.

His sister had been in a similar situation not too long ago, and his dad still hated himself for cutting her off. They'd patched things up since then, but Flynn had a feeling once Reese Gillian heard her tale he'd rethink his decision to boot her out.

"Your brother Maverick's getting married, isn't he?"

That was the absolute last thing he expected to hear, but he nodded. "Yeah."

"That's what I thought." She lifted a hand, pointing a finger at him. "Don't move."

And then she was gone with a flick of her brown

hair, leaving the scent of her—roses—behind. Flynn stood there wondering just what the heck he'd gotten himself into and why he had a feeling his life would never be the same again.

"Where is it? Where is it?" Amy muttered to herself, opening up drawer after drawer in the tiny little desk to the right of her couch that served as a command center for her fledgling business. "There it is."

She pulled out a flyer, holding it aloft before turning back to the front of the house.

Pregnant.

She skidded to a stop, lifted a shaking hand to her mouth, sickness threatening to derail her as she stood at the front door, hands over her flat belly. Pregnant with Trent's baby.

And he didn't believe it was his.

For a moment the pain from her heart breaking in two swamped her insides like storm surge from a hurricane. She had to rest her head against the front door. It wasn't that she loved him anymore. Oh, no. Trent had taken that love and bludgeoned it to death the moment he'd admitted his affair with Tiffany. It was that he'd accused *her* of being unfaithful—*her*, when all she'd ever done was bend over backward to make Trent happy.

Her fingers began to ache and it was only then that she realized she held on to the knob for dear life. She didn't have time for self-pity right now. She had to pull herself together. She needed a roof over her head and she had an idea as to how to accomplish that.

Several deep breaths later, she pulled open the front door, relieved to spy Flynn Gillian still standing there, all tall, dark and handsome and so kind and thoughtful that she couldn't stand the thought of him thinking her a complete loser.

"Here." She waved the brochure. "Look."

He seemed puzzled. She didn't blame him. Poor guy probably thought she was crazy.

"I'm a wedding planner." She thrust the trifold pamphlet at him. "I could do your brother's wedding. You know, in trade or something. Or until I get paid by my client. Or however you want to work it."

The dratted man shook his head. "Nah. I don't think—"

"No. Please. Let me finish."

She'd never taken a dime from anyone. Not once. She'd been out on her own since she was seventeen years old. Five years, she'd made it on her own—first college, then opening up her business. Five years and she'd done all right.

Until Trent.

She inhaled again. Enough. No more tears.

"I'm a good wedding planner." She grabbed his hand, meaning to place the brochure in his palm, but a charge of static electricity zapped them so that she let him go in surprise. She wondered if he'd felt it, too, but when he didn't say anything, she plunged ahead with her speech. "I have a degree in hospitality. I've done half a dozen weddings already. I'm known for whimsical weddings. See, that's the name of my business. Whimsical Weddings. I don't do the standard here-comes-the-bride stuff. I do things like tracking down the only pumpkin-shaped carriage in the western United States and arranging for my bride to be dressed like Cinderella, that kind of thing. Here."

And this time he took the brochure. She couldn't contain her relief.

"I'm a wedding planner," she said again. "And I'm super creative. Ask Mrs. Donatello. Her wedding went off without a hitch, and it was beautiful. We did this whole fairy-and-cherub theme for her wedding. Lots of tulle and toadstools. Super cute. I could do the same for your brother."

He didn't even look at the paper she'd handed him. "I'm not sure my brother wants tulle or toadstools."

"No. Of course not. We'd do something different. But please ask. I'll do anything. I'll take pictures. Or decorate. Or cater the event. Whatever you guys need."

Finally, he glanced at her brochure, but it clearly didn't help to convince him, because he barely even looked at it before meeting her gaze again. "I'm sure my dad will give you more time for the rent. Once I explain to him what's going on, he's not going to want to boot you out. There's no need to go to all this trouble."

"That's just it." She took a step closer. "It's no trouble at all. It's what I do."

"Yes, but still—"

"Please." She placed a hand on his chest. He stared at it for a moment before taking a small step back. "Just talk to your brother. And your dad."

He didn't look like he wanted to, but he nodded. Amy was so relieved she found herself smiling for the first time that day.

"Thank you," she said. "Thank you, thank you, thank you."

Chapter 2

"So let me get this straight," Maverick said the next day, resting an elbow on a stack of hay he'd just piled in the corner of their feed room, the shirt he wore nearly the exact same color as the wooden walls. "You want me to let a perfect stranger plan my wedding to Charlotte."

Flynn ignored the twinkle in Maverick's blue eyes and hefted another bale out of the bed of their truck. They'd backed into the barn, tailgate open, the feed stall already half-full.

"Yup."

His brother waited until he'd grabbed another bale, stacking it atop the one Flynn had just set down before answering.

"Well, you know this whole wedding thing isn't my deal. You'd have to talk to Charlotte."

They worked in tandem—pull a bale out, stack it, repeat. This time Flynn took his time to answer. When they'd done another five, he tipped his hat back, thrusting his hay hooks into the top row of bales. He loved the nutmeg-like smell of alfalfa that filled the air thanks to the fresh-cut hay.

"But you're not against it, right?"

"Well, hell." Maverick did the same, thrusting his hooks in the sweet-smelling hay. "I don't have a problem helping someone out, as long as Dad's okay with it."

"He told me since I made the agreement, the whole thing is now my problem."

Maverick smiled. "Sounds like Dad." His blue eyes scanned the skyline beyond the barn's opening. Flynn's gaze followed his brother's. Looked like rain. Smelled like it, too.

"So you'll talk to Charlotte?"

"Sure."

He didn't think they'd bite, and that was just as well. He didn't want to make Amy work for his family. She had enough on her plate. Eventually she'd get paid by the woman who owed her money. Until then she could just rest or something.

But, much to his surprise, Maverick sent a text later saying they'd like to see a proposal, and that Charlotte was actually excited by the idea. Flynn wasn't sure how he felt about that. It meant having to deal with Amy again, and for some reason he really wished he didn't have to.

He ended up taking the coward's way out, sending her a text message by using the number on her brochure. She replied almost instantly.

Be over in a jiff.

A jiff. He hadn't heard that expression in years. It made him smile, but his grin quickly faded. Be over for *what*? He had a busy day ahead. Big cutting horse show in a couple weeks. His dad was counting on him to have Yellow Fever ready to ride in the futurity. Then there was that stallion owner he wanted to talk to. Convincing the man to let him stand his horse at stud would be the first step toward his dream of starting a stallion station at the ranch. The last thing he needed was another responsibility, but he supposed he only had himself to blame.

She was as good as her word, the old beat-up Nissan she drove rattling down the road and sounding like her bumper might be ready to fall off. He'd noticed it the other day. She'd been rear-ended at some point and had used duct tape to fix it.

"I'm so glad I spotted you in here. In my rush to get over to the ranch I realized I didn't even ask where to find you."

She'd parked in front of their barn, a Spanish-style stable made to look like it belonged in a different era. It was the centerpiece of the ranch, nestled as it was amid rows of vineyards. His dad's place and his aunt and uncle's place stood on a hill above the stables, and on this cool and cloudy day he would imagine they had a good view of the storm rolling into the valley and Amy driving up.

"Here." She thrust a sheaf of papers at him, the horses peering at her curiously. He had to admit she looked better today than she did yesterday, less teary eyed and more in control of herself and her emotions. And yet when she stood in front of him, long brown hair pulled back off her face, there was still a hint of sadness in her eyes that made him want to… He didn't know what it made him want to do.

"What's this?"

"It's just some information on my business. Goes over my scope of work, references, that kind of thing. I wanted to see the place before I work up a formal proposal with some solid ideas on what I think might work as far as themes and whatnot. I've never been out here before."

"No?"

She shook her head. "Your dad met me at your rental property, and I mailed in my check."

"It's not mine."

He didn't know why he said the words or even what he meant by them, but he saw her brows lift.

"What's not yours?"

"The ranch. The rental property." He shrugged. "I'm employed by my dad to train his horses for competition. I don't even own my own place. I live in a cabin down the road a bit, one I used to share with my brothers, and it's owned by my dad and uncle."

She didn't say anything, just peered up at him, and he could tell she was trying to figure out where he was going with this.

"So you work for your dad?"

But it wasn't said in a negative way. She actually looked amused. She probably thought he was trying to warn her off or something, and maybe he was. Hell, she wouldn't be the first person to want to bag a Gillian brother.

"My dad's my biggest client. But I train horses for other people, too. A few of them are here."

"A few of what are here?"

Man, he wasn't making any sense. "The horses I ride."

"So you're a horse trainer?"

He nodded, wondering if he should tell her about his plans for a stallion station. "When I'm not collecting rent for my dad."

Her smile faded a bit, his words clearly a reminder of the trouble she was in. She squared her shoulders.

"I was thinking I could save your brother a ton of

money if they get married here. That's why I thought I should see the place."

She put a brave smile on things. He'd give her that.

"I think that's kind of what they want to do. But I don't know. I really wish they were here. They should be talking to you, not me."

"When are they getting married?"

"Maverick mentioned a spring wedding."

"Well, good. That gives us some time. Mind if I walk around a bit?"

"Why don't I give you a tour instead?"

And why'd he go and do that? He should let her walk around on her own. What was it about her that always made him say and do the unexpected?

"Sure," she said.

"Let's take Old Greenie."

"Old Greenie?"

"Our ranch truck. Well, it's an ATV that looks like a truck. A miniature truck."

Her face had lit up at the mention of a tour, and the relief in her eyes—that did something else to him, something he couldn't immediately identify. He found himself staring at his toes again.

"That sounds great."

He couldn't look at her as he pointed to the back of the barn, and the arena out past the barn's double doors. "It's over there."

"Let me grab my notepad first."

"I'll meet you there."

Like it or not, her troubles were now his. Lucky him.

Her hands shook.

Amy recognized the signs of impending sickness by now. After two weeks she'd developed a close, personal relationship with her toilet. Only there was no toilet in sight.

You can do this.

She focused on her surroundings—on the gorgeous stucco barn with the red tile roof and the fancy stalls inside. Wrought iron bars kept horse heads in, brown eyes peering at her curiously as they walked by.

Her stomach rolled.

And the vineyards. Those would make a spectacular backdrop for a wedding. So would the hills in the distance and the grass-covered pastures she'd passed on her way into the ranch.

Not now. You are not allowed to be sick.

He was right where he'd said he would be, waiting for her in some kind of vehicle. She smiled and waved. That turned out to be a big mistake because the motion of her arm set off something in her head. The world began to spin. Or maybe it was walking. She didn't know, didn't care, just dived to her left, pushed past some patio furniture and some chairs, hurling the meager contents of her stomach onto the rose bushes that grew along the back of the barn.

"Are you okay?" she heard him ask.

She lifted a finger, hoping he'd get the message to just leave her alone for a sec. She knew it would pass. She'd thrown up enough times that she knew the drill. She'd feel better after—weak, but better.

"Here," he said when she straightened. He held out a water bottle.

She tried to say thank-you, couldn't get her throat to work properly and ended up taking the bottle from him. Her hands shook so badly she could barely open the thing.

"Sit," he ordered.

She sat, rinsing her mouth out a few times, her first swallow of water a cold splash to her insides. And now that her nausea had passed, her cheeks began to sting in embarrassment. Or maybe that was just the blood rushing to her head. She still felt a little woozy.

"When was the last time you ate?"

She took another swallow before saying, "I had some broth this morning."

"Broth? You need to eat more than broth."

"Yeah. I know," she said, brushing stray wisps of hair away from her face, so mortified it was all she could do not to dash back to her car. "But easy for you to say. You're not the one tossing your cookies every hour."

When she met his gaze she wanted to cry, and it had to be another side effect of her pregnancy. She'd never been such a watering pot. Never. And yet for the second time in as many days she felt tears begin to build in her eyes. She was such a colossal boob. Not only did she have terrible taste in men, but she had terrible timing, too. Who threw up in front of a perfect stranger?

"Come on," he said, holding out a hand.

"I don't think I'm ready for a tour just yet."

"We're not doing the tour. I'm going to take you to my place, cook you some breakfast, get some color back in your cheeks and *then* we can go on the tour. You look about ready to pass out."

Actually, she just wanted a nap. In a sunny spot someplace, preferably with some blankets, definitely with her favorite pillow.

"That's okay. You don't have to do that."

She'd already been a big enough burden, and the man had been more than kind to her. Actually, he was a saint.

"I know I don't have to, but you're coming with me just the same." He wiggled his fingers, his meaning obvious.

She stared at his hand for a minute, at the breadth of it, at the thickness of his fingers, at the dusting of hair across the top of it. A masculine hand.

She took it.

He grabbed her notepad from her, helped pull her up, but it wasn't enough to keep her steady. She found herself falling toward him. His arms surrounded her before she could blink and she stood there in them, a sense of comfort overcoming her and making her lean into him and close her eyes.

She could have stayed there forever. He was so *warm*. And helpful. And tall.

"Thank you," she mumbled.

"It's okay."

His words were a rumble beneath her ear, his arms a haven that soothed her troubled soul. A part of her realized that she had no business leaning on him like this, that she'd only just met him, that she was taking advantage of his kind heart.

And he was kind. And thoughtful. Where had he gotten that water from? What would she have done if she'd been off all on her own touring the ranch? They probably would have found her asleep beneath some grapevines later on.

She didn't even realize she was quietly crying until he began to pat her back, muttering, "There, there."

It was like aliens had abducted her emotions. She knew she needed to pull herself together but couldn't seem to stop from crying all over his fancy Western shirt. When she pulled back a long while later, the dark denim was stained nearly black.

"I'm so sorry," she said.

He stared down at her and the weirdest thing happened. Her heart began to do something strange. It was like bird wings were tickling her insides. And the longer she stared at him, the worse it got. Eventually a whole pack of woodpeckers hacked at her rib cage.

The look on his face began to change. She saw it happen, too. His eyes went from soft and sympathetic to sharp and nearly hard, and it did something to her to see him stare down at her like that, something that shouldn't be happening given she was pregnant and prone to tossing her cookies on an hourly basis.

"Let's get you fed," he said, turning her toward the ATV.

Yes. Food. Maybe that would restore her sensibilities because the way she felt right now she couldn't possibly be in her right mind.

Chapter 3

What was he doing?

He should be working, not carting around a pregnant woman. But the look in her eyes…

He shook his head, helping her into the ATV, closing the tiny door and sealing her inside. His palms were sweaty, and if he didn't miss his guess, her hands shook. She was in no condition to tour the ranch, much less be left on her own. Her skin was the same color as his brother Carson's had been back when he'd fallen off Rooster and broken his elbow.

"You really don't have to do this."

Her tearstained face was all he needed to confirm that, yes, he did. She needed food. Maybe a warm blanket. Something to drink. Orange juice or something to help get her blood sugar up.

"I'm only a couple minutes down that way." He waved out past the arena, to the south end of their property. "Honestly. It's no trouble."

"You could take me to my place, too. It's not that far away."

"We'd have to drive all the way around to the main road, then back out again. Closer to go to my place."

She slumped against the seat of the ATV, clearly miserable. And yes, he did need to work. He had horses to ride. People to call. Things to do. Taking care of her would put him behind by at least an hour, but he didn't think he had a choice.

She didn't say a word as they drove toward the single-story home he'd taken over from Carson. It used to be a bunkhouse back in the day, and so she'd be sorely surprised if she expected a big, grand place like Maverick had just built for himself down the road. But she didn't appear to notice. In fact, if he didn't know better, he would swear she'd nodded off, her head lolling back against the seat.

"Amy?"

She started awake. She *had* been asleep.

No way.

"Wow, that was fast," she murmured, wiping at her eyes.

"Did you fall asleep?"

"What?" She sat up straighter. "No. Of course not."

But was that a hint of guilt he spotted in her green eyes? The realization that she had indeed fallen asleep raised his level of concern. There had to be something more wrong with her than mere pregnancy. Nobody could go to sleep so quickly. But she'd just been examined by a doctor. Maybe he should talk to his sister, Jayden. She was six months along right now. Surely she could tell him if Amy's behavior was normal.

"Do you need help?" he asked, slipping out of the vehicle. He'd text Jayden when he got inside.

She shook her head, then clearly wished she hadn't, clutching the dash of the ATV.

To heck with it.

He went around to her side of the vehicle, opening the door. She stared up at him miserably. He reached for her without thinking.

"What are you doing?" she yelped when his hands slid behind her back.

"Carrying you inside."

"You don't have to—" She covered her mouth, eyes suddenly going wide.

"Close your eyes."

For once, she did exactly as told. She weighed next to nothing. Surely a woman carrying a child should have body fat or something. He tried to think about Jayden, his sister, and what she'd looked like when she'd been a couple months along. As far as he recalled, she'd had more meat on her bones than Amy. His brother Shane's wife, Kait, had mentioned something about always wanting to sleep when she'd been pregnant with the twins. Jayden had mentioned that, too. So, maybe this was normal.

He somehow managed to open his front door with her in his arms, using his rear end to nudge it open. His cabin still smelled like bacon from this morning's breakfast. He headed straight for the couch to the right of the door, nudging back the coffee table his brother Carson had made, which weighed a ton, so that he could have more room to set Amy down.

"What a cute place," she said with a sunny smile meant to hide her embarrassment, or so he presumed. That and humiliation.

"Used to be a bunkhouse," he offered, going into the kitchen to his right. He opened an early-1900s-style refrigerator, or so it appeared from the outside. The whole place had been decorated by his sister-in-law's mom in a Southwestern, Art Deco–type style. Wasn't his cup of tea, but until he could afford to build his own place, he was grateful for the roof over his head.

"What sounds good? Eggs? Pancakes? Waffles?"

"You don't have to cook for me."

"You're not having broth," he said, pulling out a small basket of strawberries and a carton of orange juice. "You can snack on this while I make breakfast."

"Really, it's okay."

He poured her a glass of juice and dumped the strawberries in an aqua-colored bowl that matched the rest of the decor in the kitchen, including the tiles on the backsplash. When he set the bowl down on the coffee table, she appeared even more uncomfortable than before.

"I'm feeling better."

She lied. There was no way she could be that pale and feel any different than before.

"Eggs it is," he said, turning back to the kitchen. "And some bacon. You need fat." And before she could protest, he turned back, holding up a hand. "Not another word."

She listened, settling down on his couch. He told himself he was only keeping the best interest of the ranch at heart. That was why he was helping her. God forbid she pass out and conk her head on something while on their property.

That was what he told himself.

It didn't take long for the smell of bacon to permeate the house again. He brewed a pot of coffee, too. She didn't say a word and when he peeked a head into the family room, she'd rested her head against the back of the couch, and for a moment he thought she might be asleep again. He didn't move, suddenly intrigued with how her brows swept upward like the wings of a flying hummingbird. She had olive-colored skin and he wondered if the amazing color of her eyes was a family trait. They were like olivine stones with flecks of blue in them.

What are you doing?

"Breakfast is ready."

Her eyes snapped open. Not asleep, then. Maybe just dozing. Her gaze flicked around the room.

"Do you want me to bring you a plate?"

"No, no." She shifted. "I can walk."

Still, he kept a wary eye on her, noticing the way she swayed on her feet for a bit. She gave him a gamine grin, but he knew it was all an act.

"Wow." She paused and closed her eyes, tipping her head back and inhaling. "This smells *so* good."

He almost laughed. There was such a look of delight on her face that it could have been a seven-layer cake in front of her.

"Have a seat."

She wasted no time in sitting and digging into her plate of scrambled eggs and bacon, and he sat down across from her and simply watched. She ate with the zeal of a five-year-old.

She paused long enough to ask, "You're not going to eat?"

He shook her head, biting back a smile. "I already did."

She nodded and went back to eating again, saying between bites, "The thing about pregnancy is that really strange things begin to happen. I mean, you can toss your cookies one minute and be ravenously hungry the next." She shook her head. "And you're so sleep deprived you could probably take a nap beneath the engine of a 747. And my sense of smell. It's incredible." She shoveled in another bite. "I was driving down the road when I started to smell a cigarette. I couldn't figure out where it was coming from. But then I realized the car in front of me had its window down and I could smell the person smoking inside." She nodded in emphasis. "But we were driving down the road. I mean, like, fifty miles per hour and my windows were all rolled up but I was suddenly smelling the smoke inside my car."

He felt his brows lift.

"I know, right? I didn't make the connection that it was because of my pregnancy that I could do that until the doctor told me yesterday when I learned pregnancy turns you into some kind of superwoman bloodhound." Half the orange juice was gulped down in a few seconds. "But I'm so tired all the time. I hate it. I have a Christmas wedding that I'm planning. I love Christmas. It's my favorite time of year and I've really been looking forward to it. Now I'm wondering if I'll sleep through the holiday."

"You want some more?"

She looked down at her plate as if surprised to note she'd eaten everything on it. "Oh, uh, no. That's okay." She set her fork down. "It was really good, though. I feel so much better."

She looked better, too. The spectacular green of her eyes was illuminated by the window behind him. It had darkened outside, the air having grown thick with moisture. No doubt about it—rain was on the way.

"We should probably get going."

Just then, he heard the first fat plops of moisture on his roof. She looked up. He did, too, as a slow pattering turned into a soft drumroll, one that grew louder and louder.

"I don't think we'll be taking a tour anytime soon."

He got up, peering out the kitchen window. It was pouring.

Son of a—

"Doesn't change the fact that I still have chores to do back at the barn," he murmured more to himself than to her.

"Perfect. Let me help."

When he met her gaze, he realized she was serious.

"I mean, I don't know anything about horses, but I bet I could brush them and stuff. Or pick up the poop for you."

Pick up the poop?

"That won't be necessary."

"No. It's perfect. I can help out while we wait for it to let up. You can answer questions about your brother and future sister-in-law. That way I can start formulating ideas."

"Why don't I just call them and see if they want to come over?"

"You could do that, too."

Except Charlotte was at work and he'd bet Maverick wouldn't want a thing to do with planning his own wedding.

"Come on," he said. "Let's head back to the barn." He put the last of the dishes in his sink. "I'll text Charlotte and Maverick and see if they could meet us."

And Jayden, too, because he was back to thinking that being pregnant couldn't make someone that sleepy and hungry.

Turned out he was wrong. He had his answer before they even walked out of his house. His sister texted back three words.

Yes. It. Can.

He shoved the phone back in his pocket. *Great.*

Amy watched as he frowned down at his phone before tucking it into his back pocket. Probably his girlfriend. A man like him probably had women coming out his ears.

"We'll have to make a run for it," he said, handing her an oversize jacket and placing a black cowboy hat on his head. "Once we get into the ATV we should be okay, though. The sides will protect us."

She didn't want to leave the house. If she was honest, she would have been happy to stay there all day. Who was she kidding? Right now all she wanted was a blanket and a fluffy pillow and preferably a warm fire.

They both made a dash toward the ATV, Amy grateful for the windbreaker he'd given her to wear. It had a hood and she pulled it up over her ponytail as she ran down a river-rock pathway. She dived for cover inside the ATV. Flynn did the same thing, the two of them sitting there for a moment to catch their breath and shake water off themselves.

The jacket smelled like him, a musky scent tinged with pine and maybe vanilla. She leaned her head into the collar. Nope. Not vanilla. Talc.

When she glanced over at him she realized he watched her with an odd expression on his face. She straightened guiltily.

"Whew," she said. "It's really coming down."

He didn't say anything, just looked away and then started the ATV, pushing some buttons a second later. A single-blade wiper began to move and the warm blast of heated air hit her square in the face.

"Forget taking a nap in your house. I'll just cuddle up here for the rest of the day."

She tossed him a smile. He didn't return it, and even though she knew it shouldn't matter, her spirits sank. For some reason it was important to her that he like her. She didn't want him to think of her as a freeloader. She'd gotten herself into a bit of trouble, but it was only temporary.

Her stomach gurgled.

Well, some of it was temporary.

"Was that your stomach?"

The sting of embarrassment colored her face. "I think it's forgotten what food feels like."

His brows lifted. "It sounded like you might have more than a baby stashed inside there."

He put the ATV in gear and she turned to peer out the window. Baby. She still hadn't had time to get used to the idea. Trent had stopped taking her calls. It had broken her heart in a way she would never have thought possible. How could he do this to her? How had she picked such a horrible man to father her child? What the heck was she going to do?

She'd done some research on the internet last night and learned that paternity tests cost a small fortune. And even if she could scrounge up the money, there was the whole getting-Trent-to-cooperate thing to consider. She really didn't want to talk to him. It hurt too much. But she doubted he'd voluntarily submit his DNA, so there would more than likely be huge court costs.

She sighed.

How had she made such a complete muck of her life? And in record time, too. She should win a prize. Submit her name for the Most Likely to Have Ruined Her Life contest. And then there was the whole telling-her-mom thing to deal with. She hadn't talked to her mom in months, but sooner or later she would have to be told what was going on, because if she didn't, she'd never hear the end. And to think a few months ago she'd been congratulating herself on actually making something of her life as opposed to her mom.

"You know, if you'd rather do this another day, we could do that," he said. "The tour thing."

"No. That's okay." She couldn't do that. This was it. Her new reality. Wedding planner with a belly. Sooner or later she'd have to figure everything out. Might as well start now. It would only get harder with time.

"I'm serious about helping you out with your horses, though."

"They're not my horses."

"Okay. But I want to help."

He shook his head and she knew he'd probably refuse because he was the kind of man who didn't think women should do physical labor when they were in a delicate condition. Little did he know. There was nothing delicate about her. She'd worked all through high school, sometimes three jobs, managing her studies and work and saving up for college. She'd graduated with honors and secured a scholarship and then worked her tail off maintaining her GPA while holding down a full-time job with an event planner. *Work* was her middle name.

"You can brush horses or something."

Brush horses. That she could do.

"I have some calls I need to make. Maybe by the time I'm done it won't be raining."

She glanced through the front windshield. Wishful thinking.

Chapter 4

He parked "Greenie" or whatever it was called in the same spot it'd been before. It was only a few steps to the back of the barn, but her jacket looked like she'd been dunked in a lake by the time they made it to shelter.

"Whew." She turned back and stared outside. It almost seemed like a sheet of plastic covered the opening, it was coming down so hard. A horse nickered. It startled her, but he didn't seem fazed, just said, "Help yourself to the brushes in the box right there. I'll be in the office for a bit."

"Okay, sure." She'd never brushed a horse before, but how hard could it be? "Any horse in particular?"

He motioned toward the barn aisle. "Take your pick."

Why did she have the feeling he couldn't wait to part company with her? He dashed away so fast she was left standing there alone, a breeze wafting into the barn and causing her to shiver.

"Okay, then," she said under her breath, turning toward the first stall on her right. Two friendly eyes stared at her from behind bars.

"You look like you're in lockup," she told the brown-colored horse. "Equine jail, poor thing." She scooped up a brush from the box hanging on the wall. "Would you like your hair brushed? I bet that would feel good, huh?"

The first challenge she encountered was the latch on the stall door. It was like some kind of IQ test or something with a handle-like thing that flipped up and a bar that slid to the side. She'd assumed the door would swing open. She'd presumed wrong. It took her a moment to figure out it slid to the side, the stall front and the bars all one big panel. And then, when she finally slipped inside, the horse came toward her in a way that made her bolt back out and slide the door closed.

"You can't do that," she told the horse. "You have to stay back. I don't know you that well."

The animal peered at her in a nonchalant, clearly nonplussed way…at least, judging by the look in its eyes. Amy peered at the horse inside its room and wondered if she should just ask Flynn if she could do something else, like sweep or something.

"Okay, let's try this again." She shooed the horse away from outside the stall. The brown horse obediently stepped back. "Go on," she told it. "Move back."

It was as if it understood her words, backing up so that she wasn't as intimidated as before. She gingerly stepped inside, but she straightened in surprise when she spotted the size of the horse's belly.

"Dear goodness, either you swallowed a hippopotamus or you're pregnant, too."

The mare blew her breath out her nose, and Amy would swear it was a sigh.

"I feel your pain. As it happens, I'm pregnant, too."

She stuck her hand out, the mare sniffing her fingers. It calmed her fears enough that she took another step closer, her hand falling on the mare's long black mane, her warmth a complete surprise. "Do your breasts ache, too?" she softly asked her. "And I can't imagine it's easy to sleep with your stomach as big as it is."

She brought the brush up, pulled it through the mare's mane. "I'm not looking forward to the later part of my pregnancy, let me tell you."

She lifted her other hand, stroking the coat beneath the mane, the motion easing the ache in her heart. She'd have to do it all on her own. Single pregnant mom.

"Have you been a mom before?" she asked the horse. "That's the other thing that scares the heck out of me. What kind of mom will I be? I mean, look at my own childhood. I'm not exactly the poster child for impending motherhood, am I? My mom made it clear she wanted nothing to do with me when she moved across the country to Florida without even telling me. And then there's the whole single-parent thing. I can barely manage my business as it is. How am I supposed to do it while raising a child, too?"

The mare lowered her neck and Amy could tell she enjoyed her scratches and the brushing, and it was the craziest thing, because all of a sudden Amy felt better. The smell of a horse wasn't all that unpleasant. Kind of like a cross between a dog and the rabbit her best friend, Patty, had owned when she was a child.

"At least you have a nice comfy room and someone to take care of you." She scratched up near the mane and the horse dropped its head even more, nose stretching out in a way that made it clear she loved what Amy was doing. So she scratched harder. "I thought about moving back in with my mom, but I really, honestly think I'd rather do anything than that. Some things are just not worth the trouble. Still, I have to think about what's best for my baby."

She paused for a moment, her hand dropping to her belly. Her baby.

Would Trent change his mind about wanting to be a part of his or her life? How would they work out custody if that happened? What if he did the same thing to her baby that Amy's own dad had done to her? What if he never wanted a thing to do with their child? Or with her? Because as strange as it seemed, there was a part of her that hoped maybe he'd change his mind, come back to her, be there for her and their baby.

A nose softly nudged her. Amy turned in surprise, to see gentle brown eyes peering at her as if to ask "You okay?"

"Sorry," she said, wiping away tears. She moved around to the front of the horse, playing with the hair that sprouted between the horse's ears. "You're a kind-hearted girl, aren't you?"

The horse lifted its head, its nose nuzzling her jacket. "I would give anything to be you right now. Warm room. Meals. Someone to take care of you if you get into trouble." She touched her belly again, glancing down at the barely noticeable bump. "It's me and you, kid. You and me against the world. I hope I'm not making the world's biggest mistake. But I guess time will tell."

The mare nudged her again. Amy straightened, taking a deep breath.

Suddenly, she'd never been more terrified in her life.

Flynn stared at the computer monitor connected to his foaling system, watching as Amy scratched Boonie, the mare he'd bought on behalf of his father last year.

You and me against the world.

She clearly had no clue a camera watched her every move and picked up her every word. With horses as valuable as these, they couldn't take a chance something might go wrong during foaling. In another week he'd put a monitor on the mare, one that would chime an alert when she lay down to have her baby, but for now she stood calmly in Amy's arms, two kindred spirits.

"Are you scared, too?" he heard her ask. "I've got to be honest, horsey, I'm terrified."

He got up from his chair. Nobody had answered the phone at Dr. Stewart's. No reason to keep hiding in the office, eavesdropping on a conversation that was none of his business. But he paused in the doorway of his office, swiping a hand over his face. He should leave her alone. Let her fend for herself. She was a grown woman.

Except he knew he couldn't. With a certainty that both irritated and alarmed him, he knew he was in this for the long haul, whatever *this* was. If he walked away now, it'd be like finding an abandoned kitten on the road and letting it fend for itself. It just wasn't in his nature.

So he squared his shoulders and walked toward Amy. Boonie raised her head, alerting Amy that she had a visitor. She turned, dashing away tears. It broke his heart.

"I have an idea," he said.

She stepped back from the horse. He saw her gaze catch on the brush in her hand as if she'd forgotten it was there.

"My dad has lots of pictures of our place up at his house. Instead of waiting for the rain to let up, why don't I take you up there? We can peek through some pictures my mom put away while I tell you a little more about my brother and future sister-in-law. Give you a feel for who they are and all that."

"I don't know." Her hand still softly stroked the mare's face. "You said you have chores and things to do. I can help. We can talk while we work."

"My chores can wait."

But it was clear she didn't want to impose. She peered up at him with eyes full of dismay and discomfort. "Look, maybe we should just do this later."

"Nah. I'd rather get it over with."

She flinched and he realized his words had come out sounding harsh. He opened his mouth to apologize, but she interrupted him with, "Look, I appreciate your hospitality and all, but I'm starting to feel like a class-A jerk. Why don't you email me whatever pictures you've got and I'll start to work up a proposal back at home? I can bounce some questions off you that way. My email's on that brochure I gave you. Go on back to work. I've taken up enough of your time."

He was the class-A jerk, not her.

"Tell your brother and his fiancée I'll have something for them by the end of the week."

And with those words she started to walk away.

"Amy," he called out.

She stopped.

"My family's not going to throw you out onto the streets or anything. You don't need to worry about that. You can stay at our place for as long as you like."

Her thick lashes fluttered and he watched as she sucked in a breath. "Thank you, but I plan to pay my own way."

He was still standing there trying to figure it all out when she drove by a moment later.

Chapter 5

She couldn't stop thinking about him, not when she got home and opened up a new document and renamed it GILLIAN WEDDING, and not a few days later as she walked the short distance to her mailbox at the end of the main road. The rain had let up the other day and it was beautiful outside, the scent of wet earth hanging in the air. She wondered what Flynn was doing and, on the heels of that thought, what Trent might be up to.

Stop thinking about him.

She pulled down her mailbox door and spotted an envelope, one with the name Donatello as part of the return address. Her heart actually skipped a beat, and when she opened it and spotted the check inside, she let out a crow of delight. But then she went right back to thinking about Trent and what he'd done to her. But it wasn't just Trent she thought about. It was Flynn Gillian, too, and that was the strangest thought of all.

She was so busy imagining the look on his face when she would hand him the rent money that she didn't hear the vehicle approach, at least not at first. When she finally did look up, the four-door sedan had already turned off the main road and, for a split second, her heart did another cartwheel because it might be him. Trent.

Only it wasn't Trent.

It was the wrong type of vehicle, she realized. The sporty coupe was fancier than Trent's. The clouds overhead painted the front windshield with their own reflections, making it impossible to see who drove until the vehicle pulled up alongside her. The passenger-side window opened and Amy leaned down and caught her first glimpse of a woman with hair as black as coal and eyes as blue as a spring sky.

"Are you Amy?" she asked.

Amy's heart started pounding again, this time for a different reason. Was she in trouble? Had the Gillians hired someone to toss her out after all?

"Yes," she said warily.

The woman smiled. "I thought so. I'm Jayden. Used to be Gillian, but now it's Kotch. I'm Flynn's sister."

Amy straightened in surprise before bobbing back down to smile at her. "Oh, hey."

"Why don't you hop in? I'll give you a ride back to your place."

"That's okay. It's not that far."

"Hop in," the woman repeated, and Amy could tell this was a woman who didn't like the word *no*. So she slipped inside, the smell of new car making her close her eyes and dream of a celebrity wedding, one that would put her on the map and net her enough money to purchase a car just like this one.

"So my brother tells me you're pregnant."

Did the whole family have to know? She would have to have a little talk with that Flynn Gillian.

"Don't look so horrified. He only told me. Nobody else in the family knows. Well, except my dad, but only because Flynn wanted him to understand how dire a situation you were in. Flynn's really worried about you. He asked me to stop by, you know, so we can talk, one pregnant woman to another. Plus, I brought over some stuff. An herbal remedy that's helping me with nausea and some fruits and veggies and things for your fridge."

The woman smiled and Amy realized her bulging front side had nothing to do with too many homemade muffins, which was what she pictured Jayden Kotch doing with her time—making homemade food and knitting socks and volunteering her time for the PTA. The genetics that gave Flynn his blue eyes and dark hair were absolutely stunning on his sister. She had hair as thick as the horses Flynn rode and a smile that instantly put her at ease.

"You're pregnant, too."

"Almost six months." She patted her belly. "It's part of why I'm in town. Baby shower back at where I used to work."

Work? She wouldn't have thought a Gillian would have to work. They seemed rich beyond belief, but then again, Flynn obviously worked, too.

She spotted the ring then, a ginormous diamond that sparkled like a Hollywood spotlight in the afternoon light. Everything about the woman said "money," from the delicate diamonds in her ears to the softness of her jeans. Amy found herself hoping she'd look half as good as Jayden did when she was six months along, but who was she kidding? She'd probably have greasy hair and bags under her eyes from lack of sleep.

"Here we are," the woman said, pulling into her driveway. "I still can't believe how cool this place turned out. Carson did such a great job designing it. His construction business has really taken off in the past year and I can see why he had to hand off managing the farm to my other brother Maverick, the one who's getting married. He's doing most of the work these days." She put the car in Park and reached for the keys, and Amy realized the woman drove a rental car. "You should put out some decorations for fall. Some pumpkins would look cute on that porch."

She couldn't afford her rent, much less a pumpkin and/or decorations.

Thinking of her woes, she suddenly remembered the envelope she'd just received in the mail. "I have a check."

Jayden's brows lifted.

"I finally got paid for my last job. I can pay the rent and buy my own groceries."

"But you don't have to pay the rent. Flynn said you worked out a trade. And I brought you some groceries because it's the neighborly thing to do. The trunk is full of bags."

Charity. Flynn sent out a 911. *Crazy pregnant lady living at the ranch. Better bring her food.*

Jayden hadn't been kidding. The entire trunk was full of bags, the cloth kind with the name of a fancy food store on the front. And the brands inside weren't the local discount-store types of brands, either. She clearly shopped at one of those everything's-homegrown places, the ones with price tags commensurate with the value of the cars parked in the lot.

"Here," Amy said. "Let me take a bag or two."

"That would be great." And then under her breath, Amy muttered, "Looks like you robbed a grocery store."

Jayden laughed softly, hefting a canvas bag, one with something that looked like celery sticking out of the end of it. "I know, right?" She smiled sheepishly. "I think I went a little overboard."

You think?

"When Flynn told me about you, I knew I had to help." She slung the straps of the bag over her shoulder. "I was once pregnant and alone. Seventeen and married. The scandal of Via Del Caballo High. Then I got divorced not long after. Levi left me, and my dad disowned me and I found myself alone all over again. No money. Nobody to help. Scary times."

Amy had frozen with a hand on a bag. "But…you're a Gillian."

Jayden smiled ruefully. "Clearly, no one has educated you on our family's tragic past and all the skeletons in the Gillian closet." She reached into the back of the vehicle and pulled out another canvas bag, this one with potatoes. "It's a long story, one I'll share with you, but first, let me brew you a cup of that to-die-for tea."

The smell of the tea Jayden cooked up for her made Amy want to cry. Something minty and sweet and that soothed her by just its smell.

"Sit down," the woman said, and Amy felt bad because she should be the one cooking. She should be playing hostess, but she still sat. She had a feeling Jayden was used to being obeyed. Ergo the number of times Amy had told her she didn't need groceries as Jayden had unloaded them into her fridge. She'd been ignored and now she was ready for a zombie apocalypse, thanks to Flynn's sister.

She took a sip of her tea, her eyes closed as the minty goodness washed down her throat. "Oh, dear me. I've died and gone to heaven."

Jayden smiled. "Trust me, it's just what the doctor ordered. From here on out, you'll never go far without your tea nearby. It's a godsend."

Amy sat up a little straighter. "Were you sick, too?"

"Every morning, noon and night. It got so bad Colby brought me to the doctor. Colby's my husband. One of the kindest men I've ever met, and so good to me. He's the one who found this tea for me. There's something in it that helps with the nausea. Trust me, you'll thank him later."

"Do you still get sick?"

"No. It stopped for me about two months ago. Now I'm just getting bigger each day. I swear I'm carrying twins."

Amy couldn't seem to stop from touching her own stomach, the word *twin* sending a burst of adrenaline through her. Dear Lord in heaven, what if she were carrying twins, too?

"You look like you've seen a ghost."

"I think… I'm just overwhelmed." She tried not to think about all she had coming, the changes to her lifestyle, the responsibility, the panic she felt when she thought about how much it all would cost, the heartbreak of losing a man she'd loved but who clearly hadn't loved her back.

A hand fell on her shoulder. She hadn't even seen Jayden move. "It's going to be okay."

And this family. The Gillians. They were all making her cry with their kindness and generosity.

"I know it will be," she said with a voice thick with tears.

"First thing we're going to do is take you on a tour of the place. Flynn said he couldn't do that the other day. Then I'll see if I can find some pictures. Work is good. Work will give you something to focus on other than your scary future."

"Pictures?"

"So you can see what this place looks like in the spring, when the wedding is. It's so beautiful. All green and gorgeous. It will help you plan."

This woman, this beautiful woman, understood what she was going through. "Thank you."

The woman's eyes filled with warmth and understanding. "You're welcome."

Somehow, it didn't feel as if she were infringing to have Jayden Kotch take her on a tour of the place. Jayden drove her around in her sporty car, not seeming to mind the gravel roads or the mud when they left the vehicle to explore the vineyards or the lake up on the hill, ending the tour in front of her aunt and uncle's house. There was something she'd wanted her to see up there, behind her aunt's place. A special spot of some sort.

"This is amazing," Amy said, turning to stare at the valley beneath them. The recent rains and the cloudy skies had stained the earth a dark brown, the vines below starting to lose their foliage this time of year. Off in the distance she could see some clouds forming, their shadows blotching the earth. It made her think it might rain again. But for now she could imagine what it would look like in the spring, when the leaves would be a beautiful light green and the sun would cast short shadows on the ground.

"The view is pretty much the same from my father's place," Jayden said. "My aunt's house is just a little higher up the hill."

They'd passed Reese Gillian's home on their way to their current destination, a family gathering spot, Jayden had said.

"You up for a walk?" Jayden asked.

Amy felt so much better than she had in days. She didn't know if it was the yummy brunch Jayden had ended up cooking her or the tea Jayden had made her drink. Either way, for the first time in days, she felt up to anything.

"Lead the way."

"Let's peek in on my aunt first. I'll never hear the end of it if I don't at least say hello."

She set off toward the house, a gorgeous single story made to look like a Spanish villa.

"Come on. If you're going to be organizing Maverick and Charlotte's wedding, I should probably introduce the two of you, anyway. My aunt is about the nicest human being on the planet and my uncle is devoted to her. A real love story. You'll adore them."

Amy was starting to think every member of the Gillian family was pretty stellar.

"Will she mind us barging in on her?"

"My aunt?" Jayden shook her head, a smile making her eyes light up. "Never. She'll probably insist we stay for dinner or something."

Just the mention of the word *dinner* had her stomach grumbling again, which was ridiculous. She'd already had more to eat in one day than she used to eat in two. When the door swung wide a moment later, and the smell of something remarkable wafted out, her belly rumbled yet again. Both women froze. Amy felt her face flush.

"Goodness," said a woman with long gray hair and skin so smooth and so unblemished by time that it was hard to gauge her age. "Did that come from you?"

Amy lifted a hand. "Guilty."

"Auntie Crystal, this is Amy. She's renting the cottage from my dad, but she's also a wedding planner, so she's working on Maverick and Charlotte's wedding for us, too. I thought I should let you know that I'm taking her up the hill."

"Are you hungry, child?"

"No, ma'am," Amy said. "Jayden and I already ate. My stomach's just been acting weird lately."

The aunt tipped her head to the side. She studied her up and down, and Amy wondered if she knew she was pregnant.

"Maverick and Charlotte hired a wedding planner, huh?" A smile had burst onto the woman's gorgeous face. "How perfect."

"Well, not really," Amy felt obliged to say. "I mean, I am a wedding planner, but I just sort of volunteered my services. It's a long story."

"One I'd be interested to hear."

"We're just going to head up the hill for a bit."

"Well, you better hurry," Aunt Crystal said. "Looks like it might start raining again."

As if on cue, the earth around them darkened. Amy looked up. A giant cloud had appeared out of nowhere, casting everything in shadow.

"We'll pop in after," Jayden told her aunt.

Amy waved as they both turned and headed toward a path off the main driveway. The door closed behind them, but Amy couldn't shake the feeling they were being watched.

"Does she know I'm pregnant?"

"I don't think so," Jayden said. "And don't worry." She laughed a little. "Your secret's safe with me."

"It's just so embarrassing," she admitted. "I thought I had my life together, you know? Put myself through school, found a guy I thought was Mr. Right, started my own business. And now…"

"You're terrified of what the future holds."

"To say the least."

Jayden stared at the path in front of them. "I'm not going to lie, it won't be easy. You might have some tough times ahead, but you'll pull through." She reached out a hand and touched her forearm in a gesture of kindness that made Amy swallow a lump in her throat. "Plus, you have Flynn in your court. Did you know he's been driving by to check on you? Looking for signs of life, he called it. He's been worried about you. And once Flynn makes up his mind to help someone out, he does it. Once, we had this really terrible rooster living on the property. That thing would attack anything that moved. My dad wanted to shoot it, but Flynn insisted we rehome it. I don't know how he did it, but he managed to find someone to take the thing. And when I was pregnant with Paisley, he was the one brother I could count on to call me every day and check on how I was doing. He might come across as gruff, but he has a heart of gold. All my brothers do, actually."

Amy stopped for a moment, taking it all in. Jayden stopped and turned, too.

"It's going to be okay," she said, gently clasping her hand.

"I hope so."

"It will."

She turned, headed back up the path again, Amy following behind. She'd been lucky, Amy thought. Lucky to have landed at Gillian Ranch instead of some place owned by a slumlord who wouldn't care if she ended up on the streets. She closed her eyes for a second and thanked God above for that. When she opened them again, she stopped dead in her tracks. Jayden didn't say anything, clearly expecting her reaction. Before her stood the most magnificent oak tree she'd ever seen, one with a trunk so wide it was hard to fathom how long it'd been growing. Centuries, probably.

"It's amazing," she said.

"Maverick told me this tree is special to them."

"I can see why."

And in an instant she knew what she wanted to do. Lights. Hundreds if not thousands of lights strung throughout the branches of that amazing old oak tree. Nighttime. Softly lit. More lights, but not as many, strewed through the low-lying shrubs around the pathway. Maybe weeping willow lights for the old tree, too, the kind that hung down in thick strands. Or the altar. She could set one up beneath the old branches. It would look like a constellation of stars had landed in the meadow, a bit of heaven on earth.

"You've had an idea."

She smiled. "I have."

"Care to share?"

She smiled in bemusement. "Not yet. Not until I work it all out, to see if it can even be done. I don't suppose we could get power out here somehow."

"I'm sure we could. Generators, extension cords, whatever you need. My brothers would work it out."

"Great."

And maybe a lit carriage, too. Ooh. And the horses lit up somehow.

"Can you wind lights around a horse's legs?" she asked.

Jayden's mouth dropped open. "Well, I don't know. They have those battery-operated lights now. We could probably use vet wrapping to hold them in place. You should ask Flynn."

He'd probably think she was crazy, but that was the whole point of her idea. It was her job to take a wild fantasy and make it come to life. She'd just have to sell Maverick and Charlotte on the idea, although if she did her job right, gave them enough visuals to get an idea of her concept, the idea would sell itself.

"I don't think I need to see the rest of the ranch. This is the spot. This one right here."

Jayden's smile was huge. "I thought you might say that."

"Thank you," Amy said. "You and Flynn, you've been so kind to me." She turned, once again taking in the beauty of the valley beneath them. Rain hung down from a cloud in the distance. "I promise you won't regret allowing me to do this."

"I have a feeling we won't." Jayden followed her gaze. "And that Maverick and Charlotte will be lucky to have you." She reached out a hand and touched her again. And for the first time since she'd found out she was pregnant, Amy wasn't as terrified. Things would be all right. She could do this…with the Gillians' help.

Chapter 6

He told himself to stay away. That Amy Jensen's health and well-being were none of his concern, but the minute he said the words to himself he knew it was hogwash. So he'd popped by at odd hours, making sure her car had moved or that her mail had been picked up or that lights were on. Kind of stalkerish, but he didn't care. Like finding a baby bird on the ground, he could no sooner walk away from Amy now than he could let a nestling fend for itself.

Still, he managed to stay away for a couple of days, but it was Jayden who informed him Amy had some horse-related questions. He waited for her to call, and when she didn't, decided he might as well head over to her place to see how she was doing. That was what he told himself even as a little voice inside his head warned him to stay away.

He found her in the front yard, halfway up an oak tree.

"What the heck are you doing up there?"

She'd called out to him the moment he pulled up, although it'd taken him a few seconds to find her.

"Research," she called back.

"You're crazy. What if you fall?"

"I'm not going to fall," she said standing in the V of the tree trunk. "As it happens, I have a lot of experience climbing trees. I used to do it all the time when I was growing up."

"Yeah, but you weren't pregnant back then."

She looked like a little kid up there, her long brown hair streaming down her back, a smile on her face. "I'm not going to fall. I was just trying to get an idea of how many lights I'd need."

"For what?"

"For your brother's wedding."

Of course. He should have known.

"Please get down."

She might be up above him, but he could perfectly see her face and the frown she shot down at him. "I'm fine."

"Okay, then. I'll have to come up and get you."

"No, don't do that." But she didn't move. "Honestly, I'll be down in two seconds. By the time you climb up here, we'll both have to get down."

He had a feeling she might be underestimating the length of time she'd be up there, but he'd give her a minute, anyway. "How'd you get up there, anyway?"

"I used the nubs on the other side as footholds."

She took something out of her pocket. A tape measure, he realized.

"When I was little, I used to climb the tree at our apartment complex. It was a great place to sit and think." She wrapped the tape measure around one of the branches. "I love trees," he heard her say. "It's one of the reasons why I rented this place from your dad. So many trees all around me. Not like the city."

He watched as she turned and measured the length of a branch, although for the life of him, he didn't understand why. He was tempted to point out that each tree was different, but he had a feeling she would just ignore him. Once she finished measuring, she looked up and around, clearly taking stock of something.

"Please get down."

"I'm coming, I'm coming."

She actually appeared to listen this time, sitting down in the V of the tree. He went around to catch her.

"Move out of my way," she said when he held his arms up toward her.

"I'm just going to spot you."

"I'm going to land on your face if you don't move."

"Not if I catch you."

"You don't need to catch me. I'm just going to hop down."

He realized how ridiculous he sounded arguing with her about jumping out of a tree, but he wasn't going to move.

"You're pregnant."

"Don't remind me," she muttered.

"Come on down."

She stared down at him, clearly impatient with him, but also amused. He could see it in her green eyes, the farthest edges of them crinkling just a bit, a small smile on her face. She rolled her eyes heavenward before leaping down.

He almost blew it, almost sent both of them tumbling to the ground, but he somehow managed to break her fall, her arms wrapping around him as if she sensed his unsteadiness. He hugged her to him, their bodies connecting, his head telling him to let go, a tiny voice inside his head saying "Well, hello" to the way she felt up against him.

He let her go.

"Thanks," she said, peering up at him. She was so small, like a tiny surprise wrapped up in feminine curves, one that smelled like his mother's favorite sugar cookies.

"You're welcome," he said, tucking his hands in his pockets because, Lord help him, he felt the urge to tuck away a stray wisp of hair.

Pregnant.

With another man's child.

The words sat on his chest with the weight of an elephant. Pregnant and still embroiled with her ex. She was the last woman on earth he should be having lascivious thoughts about, but damned if he wasn't.

"What were you doing up there, anyway?"

"I was trying to get a feel for how many lights I'd need."

"Lights?"

She turned, faced the tree. "Picture this," she said.

But all he could do was admire how pretty her hair was. It might be brown—a totally average color—but it was thick and it smelled nice and he realized it was because she smelled like vanilla. That was why she reminded him of sugar cookies. It was coming from her hair.

"Lights." She waved her hands like Mickey Mouse doing a magic trick. "Everywhere. Thousands of them wrapped around the trunk of that big old tree up by your aunt's house. The grandfather tree, I heard your sister call it. We're talking head to toe, up and down and all throughout the branches. I found some pictures online of something similar, but it's nothing like I want to do. When I'm finished, that tree will glow like the Las Vegas strip."

"You'll probably burn the tree down."

She turned on him. "Excuse me?"

"A lot of lights will generate a lot of heat. What if you set the tree on fire?"

She frowned, but then she shot him a look of disappointment, her hands resting on her hips. "You, sir, are a party pooper."

"It's a valid point."

"If I use low-wattage lights I'll be fine. Here. Come inside. I'll show you what it's going to look like."

"That's okay. I'll take your word for it."

"No. I want you to see it. Come on in."

She trotted off before he could object and he realized he'd look like an idiot if he didn't follow. "I actually only dropped by for a second to see how you were doing. I don't have a lot of time."

"Yeah, your sister said you've been dropping by and checking on me."

Damn that Jayden. He'd been ratted out.

"Just to make sure you're okay."

"Crazy thing is I didn't hear you drive by once."

"Because I rode."

She stopped, turned.

He motioned over his back. "There's a path through the trees. You can get to the main ranch if you take a right out of your driveway, but it's not really a road. Just a trail. I use it all the time to school the horses."

Lies, lies, lies.

"It's good to get the horses out of the arena from time to time."

That much was true.

"Well, next time you ride by, stop in and say hello."

She left the front door open and he was reminded of the first time he'd seen her, sitting on the bottom step of the porch, crying.

"Oh," he heard her exclaim, excitement in her voice. "Before I forget, I have that rent check."

"Rent?" Why did he feel so discombobulated all of a sudden?

"Mmm-hmm. Didn't your sister tell you? Debbie finally paid me, thank God, although it was kind of your sister to drop off those groceries. Did you tell her to do that? If you did, I think I might kiss you."

He froze in the open doorway, scrubbed a hand over his face. "All I did was mention we had a single pregnant mom living on the property. She took it upon herself to do the rest."

She handed him the check, bowing a little as if presenting to royalty. "Last month's rent and this month's. I'm all caught up. And I have a wedding to do next week and this particular couple has been great about paying me on time, so I'll have next month's rent covered soon. And then I'll have the Christmas wedding in December, so I think I'm covered for the next few months."

But then her eyes dimmed and he wondered if she was thinking about her ex and the baby she carried, and for some reason he would never understand, he wanted to touch her.

"It would have been fine if you didn't pay us, you know. But now there's no pressure for you to handle my brother's wedding if you don't need to."

"Oh, but I do." She smiled and the grin made him happy for reasons he didn't care to examine. "Want to do it, that is."

She dashed toward the kitchen and picked up her tablet, bringing it over to him. She motioned him farther inside and he really didn't want to be alone with her, felt better for some reason with the door open behind him.

"Come on," she said when he didn't move.

He took a tiny step forward. It was enough for her to reach behind him and close the door.

"You can't see with that glare," she said. "Here. Look. By the way, that tea your sister brought me? It's a miracle worker. I only tossed my cookies once this morning."

If one could consider that an improvement, he thought, but then she was standing next to him, and he caught a whiff of her scent again, and all he wanted to do was go back outside even though, technically, he was barely *inside.*

What the heck was wrong with him?

"Can you see with the glare from the window behind you like that? Why don't you come into the kitchen? It's not as bright in there."

"No," he said sharply, too sharply. He swallowed. "That's okay. I can see just fine."

But he took a step forward, turning a bit so that the glare disappeared. It was a picture of a tree, one whose branches had been covered with lights, thousands of them. It took him a moment to realize there was a couple getting married standing in front of the massive trunk. Their forms were in shadow thanks to the dazzling display behind them.

"This is what I want to do, only I want to light up every single branch on that tree. I mean every one of them." She flipped to a daytime photo of a tree he instantly recognized as his aunt and uncle's. "See, I want to string hundreds of lights around the big trunk, then move upward to this branch here and here." She swiped to another picture. "And then hang these from the branches."

"These" were giant lit-up balls of some sort.

"It'll be like a constellation of stars or a universe, you know, just a twinkling galaxy of love."

A twinkling galaxy of love?

"And I was thinking, and this is where you come in, that we could have the bride arrive in a carriage drawn by horses. You don't happen to have one of those, do you?"

He nodded. "But it's probably not the kind of carriage you're thinking of. It's a buckboard, the kind with a flatbed behind the seat."

"Hmm. Maybe that will work. And I want the horses wearing lights, too, you see." She swiped again. "Like this."

She brought up a picture from an old movie he'd once seen.

"You want to light up the horses like in *Electric Horseman*?"

"Electric Horseman?"

"It's the movie this picture is from."

She tapped some keys and he realized she was searching for images from the movie, and then her brows shot up and he was fascinated with how her eyes seemed to glow like the lights she wanted to string through the tree.

"Exactly like that, except lights have improved since this movie was made, you know. There are solar-powered lights now and tiny battery packs. We could really do it up right, if you'd help me. And the carriage, too. Although now that I think about it, I really had my heart set on one of those romantic carriages. Or maybe a stagecoach. That would be cool, too. I'd want to light that up, too. Nothing like the tree, though. I don't want to outshine the bride when she arrives, but we could outline it like this." She switched to another picture of a carriage whose edges were outlined by lights. "I'd want to do the wheels, too, though. Is that possible? That's what I wanted to ask you about. That and lighting up the horses' legs."

She was insane. Either that or genius, but he was staring to see what she'd meant when she'd said she did things differently. This was different all right.

"So, my question to you is, do you have any horses that would pull a carriage? Or does Maverick have a horse he loves that could pull one?"

Option number one: one sandwich short of a picnic.

"First of all, the type of carriage you want would have to be pulled by two horses. Second, it's not like you can hook any old horse up to a carriage. Third, those types of carriages are very, very rare and hard to find."

"But you could train them, right? The horses, I mean. They already pull your flatbed thing, so it wouldn't be that hard. Because I really want to use horses from the ranch. That would be so special."

She really had no clue, but he'd give her bonus points for being so committed to her project.

"You never know how a horse will react to something new. Going from a buckboard to an honest-to-goodness carriage might be scary to them. We'd have to work on it."

"And that would take…what? Weeks? Months? Because we have that kind of time. We don't need them until the spring. You could train them over the winter."

"And what about the carriage? Where am I going to get that?"

"I'll admit, that is a pickle. I usually have brides rent the carriage and it comes with horses. This would be the first time I've ever had someone use their own horses.

I somehow doubt the rental agencies would allow us to use our own horses. I wonder if we'd be better off just buying our own carriage."

"Do you know how expensive those things are?"

"I'm guessing a lot, by the look on your face. Okay, so totally impractical. Good to know."

And the way she peered at him, like a teacher disappointed by something a student had said, almost made him laugh.

"Thousands of dollars. That's if you can even find one. I don't think Maverick and Charlotte would want to spend that kind of money."

"No." She appeared crestfallen. "Then we'll have to rent one."

"From whom? Like you said, most people who rent those things out to people insist on using their own animals...for a good reason."

"Leave that to me." She shut off the tablet. "The bigger question is, can we tape lights to the horses somehow?"

"Tape? Not likely. When we pull them off, it'd pull their coat off with it, too. No. You'd have to use something like veterinary wrap or something."

"That's what Jayden said. Or maybe masking tape. That doesn't have a lot of stick to it."

"And it breaks super easy, too. You need something with some flex that will stay put."

"Then veterinary wrapping it is." Her face had lit up again. "Perfect. Now all I need to do is run this by your brother and future sister-in-law, if you think they'll like it. It's not too over-the-top, is it?"

She stared up at him in such hopeful anticipation that even if he'd thought the idea terrible—which he sort of did—he wouldn't have had the heart to tell her otherwise.

"I think it's not up to me."

Her shoulders deflated.

"But I like it." Sometimes little white lies were necessary in life.

Her whole body inflated again. "Do you think? I was so worried they might not be the sparkly type."

They weren't. Charlotte was a social worker who was all business, and Maverick was the quiet, serious type, even more so than he was, which was saying a lot. He suspected they wouldn't want a whole lot of flash, but he wasn't about to tell her that.

"I think I'll text them right now and tell them I have an idea I want to present."

"Sure. Good idea."

He turned for the door, happy for the escape.

"Thanks for your help." She called out after him.

"You're welcome."

There were a million things he'd meant to ask her. Things like how she was feeling. If she needed anything. If she'd worked things out with her ex, but all he could do was head for his truck because damned if he didn't still recall, in minute detail, how she'd felt when pressed up against him.

"Damn."

Chapter 7

She'd never been so nervous in her life. Silly of her, she knew. It wasn't like her future depended on her meeting with Maverick and Charlotte. She had a wedding this weekend and another one next month, the holiday wedding that she was looking forward to starting. Silver ribbons. Lots of glitter. She'd always wanted a Christmas wedding, had even talked about it with Trent back when she'd thought he loved her.

Her stomach clenched, this time for a different reason. The terror she felt at the thought of a future raising a baby all by herself…well, it kept her up at night. Work had helped. It gave her something to focus on, but in the in-between moments, those seconds when her mind went quiet and she had time to think, the fear launched itself at her like a hungry tiger.

This morning, though, she'd be meeting Maverick and Charlotte, two people who'd been impossible to pin down before now. She'd been bouncing emails back and forth between them, however, and so she felt like she'd gotten to know her new clients. Or maybe not her new clients. It remained to be seen if they'd let her help them with their wedding.

She had to drive by the stables to get to Flynn's brother's home, and a quick glance at the clock on her dash told her she'd be early. It hadn't taken her nearly as long to drive around to the main ranch as she'd thought. She debated with herself whether she should keep going, but found herself turning the wheel and parking in front of the stables before she could think better of it. She needed to check in with him, anyway, about the light thing.

A horse neighed as she got out of her car. He was in the barn aisle and she wondered if she'd made a mistake. He was busy. But Flynn was always busy, and yet he still took the time to check in on her.

"Hey there," she called out to him.

He was her only friend. Maybe not friend, but the only person she could talk to. Jayden had flown back to Texas after her baby shower, although she'd told her to text her if she needed anything. She'd be back in town in a couple weeks, she'd said. But it wasn't the same as having someone she could talk to face-to-face.

"Let me guess," he said, pulling on a strap, the horse he stood next to pricking its ears in her direction. "You brought me Christmas lights and duct tape."

She smiled. "No. Nothing like that. I'm on my way to see your brother and his fiancée, and found myself with a little extra time. Thought I'd pop in and see you."

It was a glorious day outside, light streaming in from behind him and casting him in darkness until she got close enough that she could make out the five o'clock shadow on his chin, his black hair peeking out from beneath his straw cowboy hat. He appeared to be getting ready to ride. He'd taken the strap he'd been pulling on and knotted it tight before turning to face her.

"Gonna wow them with your light show, huh?"

"Hopefully," she said, rocking up on her toes and forcing a smile because she didn't feel all that confident. Flynn's future sister-in-law seemed nice, but she'd had to practically pry ideas out of her. She'd begun to fear that after all her hard work they'd decide they didn't need or want her help.

"How are you feeling?"

There it was. The question he always asked her. The question she'd never had Trent ask her. Her ex had stopped answering her calls and text messages, his intentions clear. He wanted nothing to do with her or the baby.

"I'm good." She reached out and petted the horse's brown coat. He or she was so soft, and its black mane so long someone had braided off sections of hair, the ones in the middle hanging past the horse's neck.

"Have you heard from the baby's father?"

How did he do that? It was as if he'd read her mind. And for some reason, she couldn't look him in the eye when she answered, "No."

"Putz."

"Yes, he is." She fiddled with one of the braids.

"So what are you going to do?"

This was why she'd stopped in. She hadn't even known how badly she needed to talk to someone until she'd seen his truck parked in front of the stable. She didn't have girlfriends, had never gotten along with her own sex, with the exception of Jayden. She'd wanted to do something with her life. All her friends seemed content to find a man and settle down to have babies.

How ironic to find herself in the very situation they all wanted, the very thing she'd told herself she would never do until she was older and married and more settled in life. Unlike her mother, who'd had her way too young and had struggled her whole life raising her. Like mother, like daughter.

"Well, I can sue him in court and force him to take a paternity test, but other than that, I'm on my own. Unless he comes around, but everything I've read online indicates he probably won't."

"And you're one hundred percent sure you want to keep it."

Her hand moved to her belly before she even realized it. "I'm not getting rid of it. I can't. I just don't have it in me."

But that didn't mean she wasn't absolutely terrified. She'd had her first panic attack last week. They'd gotten more frequent now that Trent had gone silent.

"It's going to be okay," he said softly, the kindness in his voice nearly her undoing.

"It is?" she said softly. "I wish I had your confidence."

He stepped around the horse, stopping in front of her, and she admitted he was unlike any man she'd ever met before. More outdoorsy. Masculine. No-nonsense.

"Have you talked to Jayden? She was in your shoes once."

"I have. She gave me some great tips. Thanks for sending her my way."

But she was still terrified. Jayden had been candid about what she'd been through and how hard it'd been when she'd been on her own. She'd given her some great advice, but none of it changed the fact that she was pregnant and single.

"Hey."

She realized she'd been hanging her head. Her heart had started to race again. The panic had returned, probably because she was due to meet with his brother and future sister-in-law and she was hoping—oh, how she hoped—they liked what she'd come up with. She was always nervous before a presentation.

"It really is going to be all right."

"I just wish I had a crystal ball, you know? One I could look into and see for myself that I'm going to make it. That me and the kid will be fine. Right now I'm having a hard time believing."

He'd taken another step closer and as she looked into his eyes she wished things were different. That she wasn't pregnant and carrying a child and that her future wasn't so up in the air.

A hand touched her chin. Everything inside her stilled. The chaos inside her head faded away until there was nothing left in the world but the two of them.

"You're going to be all right. And I know that because you remind me so much of my sister. You have her inner strength. I can see it in your eyes."

She couldn't move. "Knowing your sister, that is probably the greatest compliment I've ever received."

The world went still. She forgot that they were in the middle of a barn with a horse nearby and that she had a meeting in just a few minutes. There was just her and Flynn and this buzzing in her head that warmed her up and turned her inside and out.

He looked like he wanted to say something more, or perhaps do something more, and her whole body tensed in anticipation of whatever it was. But then his hand dropped and he stepped away and she was left standing there when he turned back to his horse.

"I have to get the bridle."

It was like coming up for air after being tumbled by
an ocean wave where you don't know which side was
up and which way you were facing—that was what he
made her feel like.

"Yeah," she heard herself say. "I should get going, too."

He turned halfway. "Good luck," he said, heading
farther down the aisle.

"Thanks."

But then he stopped and her heart went all crazy
again. When he slowly turned to face her, his body was
backlit by the light streaming through the barn door
again. He became a form in shadow that didn't move
for a moment while he contemplated words.

"You're going to be all right, Amy. You really are.
You're smart and good at what you do and your heart is
in the right place. Most women would take the easy way
out and get rid of the baby, but not you. As difficult as it
may be, you're determined to tough it out. I admire that."

He turned and headed off again and she was left
standing there, her throat having grown thick, her eyes
warming with unshed tears.

Those were the kindest words anyone had said to her.

When he came back out with the bridle, she was
gone. He was just in time to see her back out of the parking area and head off to Maverick and Charlotte's house.

His hand still buzzed from the way it'd felt to hold
her chin in his hand. He'd had the thought that he'd
never felt anything so delicate in his life.

"Dumb, stupid thing to do," he muttered.

"What is?"

He turned, startling the horse he'd been about to put
a bridle on.

"Whoa there," said his dad, walking into the barn. "Didn't mean to take you by surprise."

Flynn took a deep breath. "I didn't hear you coming."

"Who was that?" Reese Gillian asked, nodding with his chin toward Amy's car.

"Our tenant. The one who couldn't pay her rent."

"But she paid it already."

"I know."

"What's she doing here?" his dad asked.

"She popped in on her way to see Maverick and Charlotte. She's presenting her ideas to them about their wedding."

"She's still doing that?"

"Yup."

He glanced at his dad, trying to see him through Amy's eyes. He could see why she'd be intimidated by him. Gray-haired and with a stocky build, his dad looked like he might have served in the military—he had that kind of commanding air about him. People said the Gillian brothers took after their mom. Flynn had often wondered if it was his grief over losing his wife that had carved lines into his dad's face. Try as he might, he couldn't remember them being there before. His mom's death had changed him. It had changed them all, really, each in a different way.

"How's he been working the flag?" his dad asked, eyeing the horse he saddled.

"Good." He started leading Vinnie toward the arena, knowing his dad would follow. "He's not as confident as I would like when I ask him to get down in the dirt, but he'll get there."

They raised cutting horses, the type of show horse that went into a herd of cattle and separated one steer out. A good horse was able to keep a steer from running back to his friends.

"Maverick told me you've been out riding with him on the trails."

"I have." He blushed at the thought of telling his dad it was so he could check on their tenant. The less he knew about that, the better.

"Good. I like a horse that can go down the trail."

Sunlight nearly blinded him, and even with his cowboy hat on, Flynn had to squint as they exited the barn. "Been helping Maverick gather and sort, too. He's been running around like a chicken with his head cut off ever since Carson shifted most of his duties over to him."

"I know," his dad said. "This place is a lot of work and I'm grateful I have you kids to help run it."

His future sister-in-law worked for Child Protective Services. That was how Charlotte had met his brother. Maverick had been erroneously listed as the father of a one-year-old, but he'd taken the child into his home despite the false allegation. Charlotte had been his caseworker. The two had bonded while caring for the child and now Flynn would have a new sister-in-law and a new niece all within a year of each other.

"I actually wanted to talk to you about something," his dad said when Flynn stopped in front of the arena gate.

"Figured as much. I recognize the look on your face. Something on your mind?"

Reese nodded. "Been thinking I'd like to make a bid for a world championship. I know we usually do the open cutting shows, but the American Quarter Horse Association has cutting shows, too. I thought it'd look good on our stallion's résumé to add an AQHA world championship to it."

Flynn rocked back on his heels. "So you want me to

start taking our horses to cutting shows as well as the breed shows?"

His dad nodded. "I know that'll be double the work. And it'll mean a lot of travel, less time to help Maverick, too, but horses have always been your passion. I didn't think you'd mind."

He didn't mind. Not really. But it would mean extra work for his brother.

Who would keep an eye on Amy?

The thought was so out of the blue and so unlike him that he winced, a gesture his dad misunderstood.

"I hate to cut back on the cutting horse shows," his dad said, "but if that would make it easier—"

"No, no. I just need to look at the breed show schedule. Maybe there's some local competitions we could attend. Markie is such an outstanding individual that I doubt it'd take me more than a couple of shows to get him qualified. And the AQHA World Show is in the fall. We could make it work."

His dad clapped him on the back. "Terrific. I knew you'd see this as an opportunity instead of a hassle."

Maybe he could get his aunt to look in on Amy from time to time, because no matter how often he told himself she was none of his business, he couldn't help but feel that she was. The woman had nobody in the world to look after her. Things could happen with pregnancy. Look at his sister-in-law Kait. She'd been put on bed rest when carrying the twins.

"Come on, Vinnie. Let's go."

But as he swung up on the three-year-old gelding, he found himself looking down the road where she'd disappeared and wondering how it was going with Maverick and Charlotte, and more important, just why he cared so much.

Chapter 8

"All right. Close your eyes."

Amy stared at Charlotte and Maverick expectantly, although the man in the cowboy hat seemed perturbed by her request. That was okay. He'd understand soon enough.

When they both complied, she turned in her wooden chair and picked up the manzanita branch she'd decorated with battery-operated Christmas lights. She gingerly set it down on the kitchen table. When she switched on the lights, she realized the effect wasn't as dazzling as she'd wanted, thanks to the picture window behind her. Fortunately, Charlotte and Maverick had plantation shutters in their massive kitchen. It was a simple matter to swing them shut, a move that caught the attention of the little girl in the playpen to her left.

"Pretty," said the child when she spotted the lights.

"Okay, open."

It was indeed pretty, and Amy smiled at the way

Charlotte's and Maverick's eyes widened. They must have seen her bring in the branch on a pedestal, but it was clear they'd had no idea she'd decorated it with lights.

"Want," said the little girl, Olivia, holding out her hands.

"No, baby," Charlotte said. "That belongs to Amy."

"Now, picture that old tree Maverick proposed to you under, the one up on the hill behind your aunt's house, lit up like this, but only better. Thousands upon thousands of lights all wrapped around the trunk and the branches."

She took them through her idea, pulling out the proposal she'd created, pointing at the pictures she'd digitally altered to give them an idea of what the meadow could look like. A picture of a horse and carriage lit up like she wanted. Charlotte had a smile on her face, seemingly enchanted. Maverick was nodding, but his expression was hard to read—at least he wasn't frowning or asking if she had any other ideas. Usually, she had a few aces up her sleeve in case a proposal fell flat, but she'd been so in love with lighting up that old tree that she'd put all her eggs in one basket.

"Normally, I would just suggest renting chairs, but I think it'd be neat to use chairs that didn't match. We could purchase them, probably for cheap. You know, odds and ends from thrift stores. No two chairs would be alike. It would give the seating arrangements a county-like feel."

"Or," Charlotte interjected, "we could ask Carson to make us some benches for the guests to sit on."

"That would be *neat*," Amy said. "Do you think Carson would do that for you?"

"Are you kidding? He's built half the furniture in

this house. He's amazing, and I'm sure he'd be touched that we asked."

"Maybe he'd make you a table to hold the guest book, too," Amy said. "What a neat memento that would be for you guys to keep."

"Oh, I love that idea, too."

"So, you like the whole thing, then?" Amy asked. "The lights and carriage ride and all the other stuff?"

"Are you kidding? I love it," Charlotte said. She smiled and Amy admired how pretty she looked with her brown eyes lit up with excitement. It was the weekend but, in gray slacks and a light gray button-down shirt, she looked like she'd just come from work. Her brown hair was pulled back, revealing tiny pearl earrings in her ears. Earlier, she'd explained what she did for a living and Amy got the feeling that she loved her job working for Child Protective Services, but it occurred to Amy that it was probably one of those jobs that called you away from home at all hours of the day and night.

"I love it, don't you, Mav?"

"I think any wedding I don't have to plan is a good wedding," said the handsome cowboy with the same blue eyes as his brother.

"Maverick," said his fiancée, swatting him in the arm.

They loved each other, and for a moment Amy felt such a terrible pang of envy she had to look away. Stupid. She shouldn't be jealous. Maybe one day she'd find a man who'd want her and her baby, despite the mistakes of her past.

"Why don't I give you a few days to think about it?" Amy said.

"No, no. I like the idea."

Charlotte reached behind her for the purse hanging on the back of the chair. "How much should I write the check out for?"

Amy felt her brows lift. "Nothing right now. I'm doing all the planning for free." Which was either the best idea of her life, or the worst, because the money would have been nice. "All you'll need to pay me for are the hard costs—the lights and cake and the flowers and whatnot. Or you could pay for them directly. Your choice. My time is free, and you won't need to pay for any of the hard costs for a month or two, although I should probably order the lights as soon as possible. That will cost the most money, and we'll need a lot of them, but I'll let you know where to buy them."

"No. We can't impose like that," Charlotte said. "I insist on paying you for your time."

"I'm doing this in trade," Amy said, although now that she'd paid her rent, she really didn't need to work for free. Still, the Gillians had been so kind to her it was the least she could do—help out Charlotte and Maverick.

"I'm still writing you a check," Charlotte said, opening the plastic flap. "And if you say no, I'll mail it to you."

"Tree," said the little girl. "Want tree."

Charlotte and Maverick exchanged glances. "I can't believe how quickly she's learning new words," Maverick said.

"Yeah, but think about how far she's come," Charlotte said softly.

Amy realized she fought a losing battle, watching as the two of them exchanged glances, making Amy wonder what silent words they'd exchanged.

"This should cover the lights and anything else you need," Charlotte said. "If you need more, let me know."

She ripped out a check and handed it to her, the amount causing Amy's brows to lift.

"You know, I have to admit, Amy, you were spot-on with this proposal," Charlotte said. "I thought for sure you'd show me ideas that involved flowers and lace and pretty pink dresses, but you didn't."

"Good," Amy said, turning the tree so Olivia could see it better. "But you really don't have to pay me right now."

"I want to. You've clearly worked hard. You should be paid for your time."

"Thank you." She tucked the check away. "And I always try to do the unexpected. It's what I hope to be known for."

"Anyone want something to drink?" Maverick got up and she realized that the Gillian men she'd met were all tall and broad shouldered, but Flynn seemed to be narrower in frame. His skin tone was different, too. More olive toned.

"I don't want anything," Charlotte said.

"Me, either," Amy echoed. The women both stood up. "If you'd like, I can leave the tree here."

"It's okay. You don't have to do that."

"No, I'd like you to keep it."

"Tell you the truth, Olivia would probably drive us nuts trying to get to it. Go ahead and take it. It's pretty enough it could be a decoration."

It filled Amy with pride to hear her say that. She'd worked so dang hard on the thing.

"Then I guess the next time I see you will be to sign an official agreement, that is, if you're okay with that."

"Of course."

"Terrific. I'll text you when the contract is ready."

"Thank goodness we won't have to do any of the planning," Charlotte said. "The number of hours I've been working lately, I was worried we'd never get married."

"Yeah," said Maverick. "Don't take this wrong, but I'm glad you were late on your rent."

Amy smiled. "I won't."

"It was nice of my brother to run interference with my dad."

"I heard he called in Jayden to help you, too."

The couple exchanged glances, and for some reason, Amy blushed. "He's been very kind to me."

"Usually, all Flynn cares about are his horses," Charlotte said, but she was teasing. They both were. Or maybe not. Did they know she was pregnant? Jayden had said only she and her dad knew.

"I can't remember the last time he went out on a date," Maverick added.

They couldn't know. If they knew she was pregnant, they wouldn't be teasing her like this—as if Flynn might be interested in her.

"There was that horse trainer out of San Diego. Remember her?" Charlotte rolled her eyes. "I was so glad when he dumped her. Huge ego. No heart."

"And then that cute barrel racer from up north," Maverick said. "But that only lasted, what, two minutes?"

"Two months," Charlotte said. "But you're more his type."

"Uh…" Amy didn't know what to say. "I doubt that."

She realized Charlotte was only trying to be nice. She even dismissed her words with a swipe of her hand. "No, you are. Pretty. Smart…"

"Pregnant."

They both drew up in surprise. Amy nodded. "Nearly

two months along. Trust me, your brother wouldn't be interested in me." She smiled and hoped it hid her embarrassment.

"Oh, gee, I'm sorry. I didn't know you were involved with someone. Flynn's been so concerned about you I just kind of assumed you were on your own."

Amy took a deep breath. Might as well confess it all.

"I am alone. The guy who knocked me up dumped me for another woman. He's convinced someone else is the father of our child, which is kind of ironic given he was the one cheating on me, not the other way around." She patted her belly. "So it's just me and Junior here. But don't worry. It won't affect the planning of your wedding. I'm not due until a couple of months after you two tie the knot."

Charlotte closed the distance between them, touching her gently. "Amy, we had no idea. I'm so sorry if we upset you. We didn't know."

And there they went again, her damn eyes filling with tears, like some kind of spontaneous spigot. Super annoying.

"No, no. It's all right. I'm flattered. I'm just… pregnant." She tried to make a joke out of it, smiling brightly. "Not many men want to date a woman who's knocked up."

"You don't know that. There might be someone."

Oh, she doubted that. Who the heck wanted to date a woman carrying another man's baby? Even if she was ready to date again, which she very definitely was not.

"Anyway, I'll get started on researching lights right away. And I'll have the contract ready for you to sign ASAP. I have a template I use. Super easy to find and replace names. I'll just have to change the payment part to reflect what you just gave me."

She was rambling, and she nearly tripped in her hurry to grab the tree, which set Olivia off, the little girl's gray eyes filling with tears, cheeks instantly flush.

"Tree," she cried out.

"Sorry, honey," she told the little girl. She snatched up her tablet and, juggling the tree, backed out of the kitchen. Charlotte scooped up Olivia in an attempt to soothe her as Maverick rushed forward.

"Let me get the door."

"Thank you," she said, but the words were barely audible because her throat had gone thick with tears, and the crazy part was, she didn't know why. It wasn't like she was about to start dating anyone, so what did it matter if they silently agreed Flynn would never be interested in her?

It did matter, though, and damned if she knew why.

Chapter 9

"What do you mean she seemed upset?" Flynn asked his brother the next morning. They were saddling up some horses to ride out and check on a sick calf Maverick had spotted early in the morning.

"We were just teasing her, you know. Talking about how you hadn't been out on a date in a long time."

"What?"

It was a testament to how guilty Maverick felt that he actually appeared a bit sheepish. "We didn't mean anything by it. Charlotte and I were just happy with her proposal and I think we both sort of thought she'd make a great girlfriend for you, and then she let the baby bomb drop and I think our reaction upset her."

Flynn rested a hand on the pommel of his saddle, trying to gather his thoughts for a moment because what he wanted to do was close his eyes and groan. Just what she probably didn't need...a reminder of everything she was facing and the fact that she didn't have a boyfriend because of her piece-of-you-know-what ex.

"We didn't mean to upset her, bro. We were just having some fun."

"She was upset?"

Maverick shrugged. "Yes. No." He shook his head. "I don't know. She just got out of there in a hurry. So if you bump into her, let her know we didn't mean anything by it."

If he bumped into her.

The whole time he rode with his brother, though, he wondered if he shouldn't "bump into her" today. There was really no reason to make a pest of himself. He was sure she was fine. His brother and Charlotte had loved her proposal. That would put her in a good mood. And yet when he finished riding, he found himself worrying about her. Not because of Maverick and Charlotte, but because... Well, just because. He'd just pop in for a few minutes, check to ensure she was all right, then be on his way.

She sat on her front porch in the exact same spot she'd been sitting when he'd first met her. She'd probably straightened up when she heard his truck because he had a feeling she'd been sitting there for a while, her purse tossed to one side, her black jacket, leggings and tall boots telling him she'd either been somewhere or was about to go someplace.

"Hey," he said, climbing out of his truck, reminding himself he would just stay for a few minutes.

"Hey," she echoed.

She'd left her hair down, wisps of it catching a slight breeze and blowing across her face. She forced a smile, but it was half-hearted at best. Even so, it changed her face in the same way sunlight could transform stained glass, her eyes brightening, her lips parting to reveal a friendly smile.

He found her attractive.

No sense in denying it anymore. Petite chin. Wide green eyes, the kind that almost seemed to change colors, and that were accentuated by wide, sweeping brows.

"You going somewhere?"

"Yes." She sighed. "No."

And once again he found himself sitting next to her and wondering what it was about her that made him want to pull her into his arms. Was it the pregnancy? Was there some kind of weird physiological thing going on? One that stirred his male psyche and roused latent protective instincts?

"What's the matter?"

She looked away from him, staring up at the tree he'd found her climbing the other day. "Doctor's appointment," she said. "I've been trying to drum up the courage to leave for the past ten minutes, although at this point, I'm going to be late and so now I'm wondering if I should even go."

"Why not?"

His heart had started to pound as he waited for her to answer. He took a deep breath, and lifted the brim of his cowboy hat. When she didn't say anything, he hooked his thumbs in his jeans.

"What's wrong?"

She took a deep breath, too. "It's just that today is the day where I'll be seeing the baby for the first time and I'm kind of freaking out about it." She smiled ruefully and looked him in the eye. "I think it suddenly hit me that this is really happening. I really have a baby inside me. I mean, I knew that already, of course I did, but I guess on some level I didn't really know that." She peered up at him in question. "Does that make sense?"

"Sure."

She huffed. "No, it doesn't. You're just saying that."

He found himself smiling. "Okay. All right. I don't have a clue what you're talking about. You're either pregnant or you're not."

"Yeah, but *seeing* him or her for the first time…"

Her words dribbled off and she looked away again, her expression suddenly sad. "Trent should be here for that."

The mention of Trent raised his hackles. "That piece of you-know-what shouldn't go near you or the baby. He doesn't deserve you."

She met his gaze again, and he could tell his words had touched her in a way that elevated his heart rate again. "Thank you," she said softly.

"No problem."

She took a deep breath. "I guess I can't avoid it any longer. Might as well set off."

"I could go with you."

What? What was he doing?

"Oh, no. I couldn't impose. I was just being a coward by sitting here. I really should get going."

She grabbed her purse. He stood up before her, offering a hand. She smiled and took it, but when he pulled her up, when she was damn near up against him again, they both froze. He saw her eyes search his own and out of nowhere came the urge to kiss her, only he knew that was a bizarre and crazy idea, so when his head dropped, he found himself kissing the top of her head instead.

"It'll be okay."

It was as if she were a toy and someone had taken the stuffing out of her. Shoulders that had been bravely squared before suddenly slumped, and before he could stop himself, he was pulling her into his arms, holding her one more time. She didn't cry this time. That, at least, was progress, but he could feel her trembling and it damn near broke his heart. No woman should have to go through this alone. The thought was a beacon in his head that couldn't be ignored. That was why he'd popped in to see her. He felt sorry for her.

"Come on." He drew back, grabbing her by the shoulders. "We are going to the doctor together."

"But...don't you have to work?"

"I'm self-employed. Sort of. I make my own hours. Besides, the horses won't mind an afternoon off."

"But I couldn't—"

"Shh." He scooted around behind her, placed his hands on her shoulders and started to guide her toward his truck. "Just tell me where we're going and I'll take you."

What was she doing?

She shouldn't be so quick to accept his offer of charity. None of this was his problem, and yet whenever he offered a shoulder to cry on, she couldn't seem to stop herself.

"Where are we headed?" he asked, turning onto old Highway 21.

"It's by the hospital," she said. "There's a medical building right next door."

He nodded, his face in profile beneath his cowboy hat. "I know the one. My sister-in-law practices medicine at the hospital."

She turned and stared out the window, at the passing trees and pastures, the grass burned brown by the California summer sun, but with patches of green coming up thanks to the recent rains. In a month or two everything would turn green. Seasons would change and by the summer she'd have a baby.

Her hands tightened in her lap. A baby and a life she hadn't planned for.

"The good news is your brother and sister loved my proposal," she said, uncomfortable with the silence in the truck.

"I heard."

She turned in her seat. "You did?"

He nodded. "Maverick needed help this morning with a baby calf. He told me Charlotte hasn't stopped talking about it. And that they're sorry if they made you feel uncomfortable there at the end."

She shook her head. "They didn't."

They lapsed into silence again and the closer they got to town, the more her heart raced. She had no idea why she was such a nervous wreck. It wasn't like today's doctor's visit would make her uncomfortable or anything, at least she didn't think so. She'd never had an ultrasound before, but they didn't look scary on TV.

"What was wrong with the calf?" she asked.

"Weak. As far as we could tell, didn't get up to nurse. We've got her in an empty stall back at the stable. Had to bottle-feed her."

"You do that? Give baby cows bottles?"

"Yup. Part of living on a ranch. Sometimes the babies need help."

And he helped them. She turned toward the window again. The man was a prince, a genuine, bona fide knight in shining armor.

As they neared the hospital, Amy's palms started to sweat. Just an easy doctor's visit. They'd confirm what she already knew and she'd be on her way. But as

Flynn pulled into a parking space, she felt the familiar tingling in her belly.

Panic attack.

Come on. Suck it up. It's just a simple doctor's appointment.

"You okay?"

"Yup, fine," she lied.

"I thought I'd go in with you."

"Nope. No need to do that." She forced herself to pull on the truck's door handle. "I'll text you when I'm done."

She slipped out of the truck and started walking toward the doctor's office before the panic attack hit full force. Today was the day when she'd finally see the baby, when it would go from a faceless creature living inside her belly, to something alive and growing and that she'd have to give birth to at some point.

Dear God. Birth. She didn't even want to think about that.

"Amy."

She'd been concentrating so hard on not hyperventilating that she didn't even realize Flynn had slipped out of his truck. That he was right behind her.

"Come on," he said, rushing ahead and grabbing the clinic's door. "Let's do this together."

She couldn't move. Her feet were stuck as she looked up and met his gaze. The urge to grab his hand was so overwhelming she had to look away to stop herself from doing something stupid.

Gratitude. That was all it was. She loved him in that moment. Not, like, *love* loved. Love like friendship love. That was why it felt as if her heart swelled to twice its size and why her whole body flushed with a warmth that filled her.

"Will you marry me, Flynn?"

It was a joke. Or it was meant to be, but for one panic-stricken moment she thought he might take it wrong.

"No, thanks. Not today." But he smiled and she knew he'd picked up on the fact that she was just trying to ease the tension.

She tipped her chin up. "Okay. I shouldn't drag you into this any more than you already are, but I can't seem to stop myself. You're a saint, Flynn. You really are. I'm naming my kid after you."

"What if it's a girl?"

"Then I'll call her Flynnanita. Either way, it's happening."

They both laughed and it felt good, it felt so dang good to have someone by her side through this. The thought instantly sobered her.

"Thank you," she said softly and earnestly.

A hand reached for her own, his big fingers squeezing her gently. The look on his face was probably the same one he wore when he was saving baby cows and rescuing evil roosters.

"You're welcome."

And she wished—oh, how she wished—Trent could have been more like him, a decent guy…someone just like Flynn.

Chapter 10

He was taking this babysitting thing way too seriously, Flynn thought, waiting with Amy for the doctor to arrive. She'd been asked to lie down on a table, her brown hair splayed out beneath her, her hands nervously fidgeting with the edge of her shirt.

"If they ask me to put my feet in those stirrup things, you do realize you're going to have to leave," she said, but the words were said with an edge of hysteria to them. "I mean, you're a good friend and all, but we've got to draw the line somewhere."

"Don't worry," he said with a reassuring smile. "If they ask you to put your feet in those stirrup thingies, I'll be gone before you take off your boots."

"Oh, goody."

But she was terrified. He could see the pulse beating at the base of her neck and for a moment he felt such a deep-rooted sense of empathy for her that it was nearly a physical ache. Her chest rose and fell, and she flinched when the door opened.

"Okay," said a female doctor who didn't look old enough to practice medicine, much less be an obstetrician. "Are you ready for your—" The white-coated woman stumbled to a stop. "Flynn." She pulled the tablet she'd been holding up against her chest. "Oh, my goodness, Flynn, I haven't seen you since high school."

Out of the corner of his eye he saw Amy glance over at him. But for the life of him he couldn't remember who the woman was.

"It's me, Christine Nelson. I helped you pass integrated math back in high school."

The blurry image of a woman with thick-framed glasses and a mouthful of braces rose up in his mind. But the woman in front of him didn't look a thing like the Christine Nelson he remembered.

"Of course I remember you," he lied. Well, maybe not. The eyes were the same.

She smiled up at him bashfully, her blond hair pulled off her face. She seemed to have forgotten Amy was in the room.

"Uh, how have you been?" he asked, glancing at Amy again. She seemed strangely amused.

"Good, good," Christine said, nodding her head. "I ended up going to medical school just like I said I would, but I changed my mind about pediatrics. I decided to be an ob-gyn instead. I'm a resident here."

"That's great."

She kept smiling at him. Flynn turned back to Amy.

"I went to school with her," he told Amy.

"So I gathered."

That was definitely amusement he heard in her voice. He could see the laughter hiding behind her eyes.

"And you must be Amy," Christine said after peering at her digital chart.

"I am."

"Amy is a friend of mine," he said with a smile, although he had no idea why he felt the need to explain. "I'm just here for moral support."

"So if you ask me to strip naked," Amy said, "he's going to have to leave the room."

Christine looked between the two of them, but her gaze settled on him. "It's so sweet of you to support a friend like this. Did you ever become a famous jockey?"

Was he blushing? Damn, the mention of riding racehorses brought back memories he'd long forgotten, and the words solidified it really was the Christine he remembered. He hadn't thought about being a jockey in years, not since he shot up in height his sophomore year.

"Not a jockey. But I do ride horses for a living."

"Oh, yeah?" Christine asked, but she looked down at Amy with a professional smile and said, "All I'm going to do is lift your shirt a little bit."

Flynn averted his eyes just in case. "My dad got into cutting horses. We breed and compete on them. I'm in charge of the horse operation."

"So still horse crazy, then?" she asked with a smile, pulling a machine toward her, one that was on rollers so that she could easily maneuver it so they could both see the screen. She pulled on some latex gloves while waiting for Flynn to answer.

"I guess you could say that," Flynn said.

Christine took a seat on a stool next to Amy and gave her another professional smile. "I'm going to put some gel on you now. It should be warm, so no worries." The doctor-to-be flipped on a screen. Flynn watched as she grabbed what looked like a showerhead and placed it against Amy's stomach.

"And your brothers and sister? How are they all doing?"

"Married," he said, looking at the screen and wondering how the heck anyone could make sense of what was displayed.

"And you? You married yet?"

"Nope," Amy answered for him.

Christine glanced at Amy quickly before meeting his gaze again, and for some reason Flynn went back to blushing. He had to look away, focusing on the screen. "Do you see anything yet?"

"Not yet." Christine focused her attention on the monitor. "Let me just move this around." She did that for a few seconds before saying, "There. Right there." She pointed to the screen with her finger. "There's your baby right there, Amy. See that light spot on the screen? And see that area flickering? That's baby's heartbeat right there."

Flynn leaned closer in amazement. He'd seen baby horses on sonograms before, but a tiny human life? This was a first. It was so small.

"You're just about nine weeks, by the looks of things," said the doctor. "Good placement of the placenta, too. Nothing to worry about there. You're all good."

When he glanced at Amy, she was back to looking scared again. He found himself reaching for her hand, squeezing it.

"It's going to be all right."

"I know," she said in a tiny voice. She stared at the screen and the tiny picture there. Suddenly things just got very, very real for her. Flynn could tell.

Christine was staring between the two of them. "Would you like a picture?" she asked.

Flynn looked at Amy, who nodded minutely. He answered for her, "Sure." And then he smiled down at her. "Our first picture of Flynnanita."

That made Amy smile, but only a little. Christine pressed some buttons and then removed the wand. "They'll print them out for you up front."

And that was that. Christine wiped Amy's stomach down before stowing away all the equipment. When she'd finished, she stood up and removed her gloves, tossing them in a bin next to the bed.

"Well, it was good seeing you, Flynn."

"You, too, Christine."

But she didn't leave right away and Flynn wondered if she had something further to say. She stood there, shifting her weight from foot to foot.

"We should get together. Catch up."

"Yeah, sure."

She stood there, waiting, Flynn didn't know what for. "Give me a call sometime."

"I'll do that."

She finally turned away, leaving the room. Flynn turned back to Amy, who started to shake her head.

"What's wrong?"

"She was waiting for you to ask for her number, you idiot."

"No, she wasn't."

Amy just rolled her eyes, tugging her shirt down, but when she sat up, her hand covered her belly and he knew she was thinking about the baby again, about what it meant for her future and everything that went along with having a child.

"What am I going to do?" he heard her ask.

"You're going to think positive and eat right and take care of yourself." He wagged a finger at her. "No more climbing trees."

But she didn't answer him. Her eyes had lost focus. "Am I making a mistake, Flynn? Should I really be having this baby right now? What if I'm a terrible mother?"

He closed the distance between them, grabbed her hand again. "You're going to be fine."

She met his gaze and that was when it hit him, that was when he realized how badly he'd wanted to kiss her earlier when she was looking so glum. He dropped her hand and stepped back, because it was insane. He'd just been staring at another man's child in her belly. He should not want to kiss her.

But he did.

"I'll bring the truck around. Meet you outside."

She stared up at him strangely. "You really should give that pretty doctor your number. She seemed nice."

"No, thanks."

Because he didn't want to give Christine his number. He wanted to tell Amy to call him.

He turned. "I'll see you outside."

Chapter 11

Flynn had been strangely quiet on their way back to the ranch. That was okay. It'd suited Amy just fine. She kept pressing her hand against her belly, as if she could feel the little life inside her. She couldn't, but that didn't mean it wasn't there. Oh, no. It was there all right. Today had confirmed that.

It was real. It would really happen. At some point early next summer she'd be a mommy.

She supposed on some level she'd wondered if the pregnancy tests had been wrong. Of if maybe she'd read them wrong. It'd been a ridiculous thought. A doctor's office and a store-bought pregnancy test wrong? Alas, that wasn't the case at all.

She'd have to call her mother.

She realized she'd been holding off on doing that until today's appointment. But now it would have to be done because if she didn't tell her now, early on in the pregnancy, she'd never hear the end of it.

Who was she kidding? She'd never hear the end of it, anyway. It wasn't that she didn't get along with her mom. Growing up, she'd had only her mother to take care of her, Amy's dad having taken off. But Amy had always felt like her mom couldn't wait to be rid of her. Almost as if she were a burden. So the moment Amy had graduated high school, she'd moved out, started college, pursued a degree in hospitality. Her mom? She'd moved to Florida without so much as a word to Amy. She'd heard about the move from a friend. Her mom claimed the job market was better in Florida, but that was a load of malarkey. Her mom had worked retail her entire life. She could find a job anywhere. So there was a part of Amy that always wondered, just a tiny little bit, if her mom had moved all the way across the country to get away from being a mom.

I won't ever make you feel that way.

She patted her belly, breathing deeply to stave off panic. She might be doing this alone, but she'd do it better than her mom ever had, that she promised the tiny life inside her.

"You okay?" Flynn asked.

She nodded, but her throat had gone thick. She would be fine. She didn't need to worry. When she'd moved out of her mom's apartment she'd been scared to death, too, but she'd managed. College. Even an internship with one of the area's biggest wedding planners. She could do this, too.

"You don't look okay."

And then, strangely, and from out of nowhere, came a sense of complete and utter calm. Her eyes stopped stinging, her throat cleared. Okay, maybe not calm. She'd just gone…numb.

"No. I'm good."

But when she glanced over at him, she was reminded of the good doctor and the way the beautiful MD had blushed the moment she'd realized she had Flynn Gillian in her exam room. Via Del Caballo royalty, she'd heard the Gillian family called. She would bet the doctor had had a crush on him back in high school. There'd been something about the way she'd peeked up at him through her lashes. She looked back out the window because Flynn deserved a woman like Dr. Nelson. Someone who had her life together and the future planned out and who'd be as kind to him as he was to everyone else. He deserved kindness.

"I think you should call your ex," he said. "Send him a picture of the sonogram."

"Why? So he could claim the picture is of someone else's baby?" She shook her head. "Because that's what he'll do. Once the baby is born I'll be able to prove it's his. Until then…"

"Can't you do a DNA test now?"

She shook her head. "Too expensive. It's better to wait until the baby is born."

"So that's it, then? You're just going to do this all alone?"

"What choice do I have?"

"Surely you have family?"

"It's just me and my mom, and she lives in Florida, and I haven't told her yet."

"Why the heck not?"

She shrugged. Because she had a feeling her mom wouldn't care. Because she didn't want to ask her for help when she didn't want her mother's help. Because no matter what she told herself, her mom taking off on her had hurt. Badly. Only now, when she was pregnant, did she realize just how wrong it was to disconnect so completely from your child. She would never abandon her kid. Not now. And definitely not when they were older.

She was so engrossed in thinking about her mother that it wasn't until he pulled up in front of her house that she realized they were home.

"You look upset," he said before she could open the door and slip outside.

"I can't thank you enough for going with me today, Flynn."

He met her gaze, his eyes dark beneath his cowboy hat, and, man, did she wish things were different. What would it have been like if Flynn had been her baby's father? How much easier would things have been? How much more secure would she feel? But he wasn't. Instead, she had to deal with a man just like her mother. Someone who put his own selfish needs first.

She let herself out of the truck, waiting to see if he'd follow. He didn't, though, and it was ridiculous how let down she felt when he started to back down the driveway, Amy waving at him as if her mind wasn't spinning and her world wasn't turned upside down by the ultrasound and her thoughts about Flynn and the ever-present disappointment in her mother. She forced herself to take a deep breath, facing her front door and her future.

Behind her she heard the truck stop moving. When she heard the door open, every muscle in her body tensed because she needed him, needed Flynn, someone to wrap their arms around her and tell her everything would be okay. She turned back just in time to see him slip out of the truck, leaving it running. He approached her slowly and she tried to tough it out, to make it seem as if everything was okay and that her world wasn't cracking open and her heart breaking in two.

"What's up?" she asked.

He tucked his hands in his front pockets and she had to lean back to look up at him. A bright blue sky framed his face and cowboy hat. His eyes were the exact same color as the heavens above.

"I just wanted to tell you that I think you're amazing." His shoulders flexed, as if he wanted to move but couldn't. "I mean, I know I've said this before, but I really admire the fact that you've decided to keep the baby."

She had to look down at the ground because she didn't trust herself to keep looking in his eyes. "If you knew how often I've second-guessed myself, you might not think so highly of me." She inhaled in shame. "You have no idea how many times I've thought my life would just be easier if I…" She took a deep breath. "If I just…"

She couldn't even finish the sentence.

A hand slipped free of his pocket and she knew what he would do before he did it, his fingers soft as he gently brushed the side of her face. It felt as if he touched her with a feather. She closed her eyes, and it seemed as if time stretched to the point of snapping while she waited for him to do…something.

"Amy," she heard him say.

She couldn't look at him. If she did, he'd see it in her eyes, the need she felt for him to do more than touch her, and she was ashamed of that need because she was pregnant and still in love with Trent. Maybe. She didn't know. The point was she carried another man's child.

But she *had* to look, had to peer into his eyes. The softness there. The kindness. The look of gentle understanding.

"What are you doing to me?" he asked.

The same thing you're doing to me, she wanted to say.

"Kiss me, Flynn, please."

His pupils flared and his face tensed and she waited for the rejection. Who would want her? Not someone like Flynn. But then his head lowered and she thought that maybe, just maybe…

His lips lightly grazed her own.

This was her yes, the yes she'd been silently saying to him. Yes, it was okay to kiss her. Yes, it scared her, too. Yes, she didn't understand it, either.

Her eyes closed again so she felt rather than saw him close the distance between them, and when he hooked a hand in the loops of her jeans and tugged her up against him, she silently cried out "Yes" all over again. His head tilted, his mouth silently asking for more. She gave it to him, parting for him, the warmth and the taste of him causing her body to warm in ways it shouldn't.

Pregnant.

She pulled away, her hands finding the front of his shirt, palms resting against him for support.

"We can't," she said.

"I know," he answered back.

But why couldn't they? a tiny voice asked.

"I should get going."

He stepped away and she let him go because there were a million reasons why this was a bad idea. He'd done so much for her and she wasn't going to drag him into her hot mess of a life. She couldn't ask him to get involved with her. Not now, not while she was pregnant. Goodness, what if his family found out? They'd probably peg her as a gold digger or something. They already had a low enough opinion of her as it was. Well, at least his father did. Probably. She didn't know. And, see, that was the problem. She wasn't thinking clearly. Neither was he. She was hopped up on some kind of

pregnancy-hormone cocktail. That was all this was. Not
the beginning of something special and wonderful and
wholly unexpected. She couldn't be that lucky.

"Thanks," she said, and it sounded pretty lame, even
to her own ears.

"I'm sorry," he said.

For what? she wanted to ask. Instead she watched
him walk away, slip into his truck again, and this time,
he actually drove away.

What in the hell?

Flynn gripped the steering wheel for all he was
worth.

What in the living *hell*?

She'd been standing there looking so sad and afraid
and so lonely and he couldn't resist. He just couldn't
stop himself. He'd had to stop the truck and get out
and…and…

He'd *kissed* her.

He banged the steering wheel again. She was *not* his
problem. He had enough on his plate without having to
worry about their pregnant tenant and how sorry he felt
for her. That was all this was, he reminded himself. Pity.
She wasn't even his type. He preferred women like that
doctor. Women who had their life together and weren't
afraid to go after something they wanted. Amy? She
was nice and sweet, but her whole life was in flux and
he should stay away because who the hell knew what
would happen in the future? For all he knew that guy
Trent might come back once he came to his senses.

Thank goodness he was headed off to a horse show.
It would make life easier. He could avoid her.

But the whole time he prepped for the show, and then
later, when he competed, he kept waiting for her to text

him or to call, and he realized he'd gotten in a routine with her, and he missed that routine. But she kept her distance and he knew he should be grateful for that. She wasn't reading more into their kiss than she should. She wasn't trying to lure him into being her baby daddy or something. She was keeping her distance.

When he got back home, though, he ached to see her, just to check in with her. In the end, he didn't have to. There was a note on his door.

Flynn,
Maverick told me you'd be back from your horse show today and that you wouldn't be home until late. I made you some food and had Maverick put it in the fridge. I'll be honest. It's a peace offering. I hate that we're not speaking, I miss my friend. So let's just forget about the other day, okay? Hope to see you soon.
Amy

He stared at that note for what must have been fifteen minutes. There it was in black and white. She wanted things to go back to the way they were before, too. Except they could never go back to that. You didn't kiss someone and just forget about the way that kiss made you feel, and right there and then he admitted that the kiss he'd shared with Amy was unlike any other kiss he'd ever had. It'd done something to him. Something crazy and unforgettable, and it scared the you-know-what out of him.

But it wasn't in his nature to avoid a problem, and so he headed over to her place the next morning. He told himself he was actually killing two birds with one stone. He would ride one of the younger horses over to her place, and on his way out he would check on the mares and foals they kept down the road from the stables. It would take much longer to get to Amy's rental, through the hills and down a dirt road, but he could check fences along the way.

Excuses, excuses, excuses.

His hands shook when he rode up to the little house his brother had built, tying the palomino gelding up to a tree. She was home, her beat-up little car in the driveway, and that sent his pulse skittering across his rib cage like it was some kind of damn bingo ball. The whole ride over he'd told himself she wouldn't be home and that he could leave her a note and then the next move would be up to her. Ha.

He heard music as he got closer to her front door. Loud, thumping music that he instantly recognized. "Jump around," the lyrics told her, and by the sound of it that was exactly what she was doing. He could hear her feet hitting the floor as she jumped, jumped, and for some strange reason he went over to her front window and peered inside. And there she was. Jumping up and down, head swinging side to side to the music, feet hitting the floor so hard he could hear dishes clattering in the kitchen. She bounced like Tigger, up and down, up and down, brown hair flying as she swung around, a silly smile on her face, and he didn't know why, but the sight of her bouncing around, carefree and happy, made a warmth settle in his chest, and he could have stood there watching her all day.

She spotted him.

The music played on, but she froze, eyes wide. And then she began to laugh. Just laugh and laugh even though he couldn't hear her over the sound of the music and through the window. She went over to her phone or whatever it was that sent music to her speakers and he turned toward the front door. She swung it open right as he stopped in front of it.

"Enjoy the show?" she asked with a wide smile.

The urge to pull her to him, to kiss the irreverent smile off her face, to hold her up against him and absorb some of the joy she seemed to exude, well, it was so overwhelming he had to clench his hands to keep from doing it.

"You should charge admission."

Do it, a little voice said. *Kiss her.*

He couldn't. Wouldn't. Like he'd told himself a hundred times before, he had no idea what would happen once Trent figured out she was telling him the truth. What if he came to his senses and decided to come back? What if he let himself feel things for her, crazy things, only to be shown the door when the father of her child came back into her life?

"I don't know why, but I felt the need to dance."

"Well, I'm glad you're feeling better. The other day…"

When we kissed.

He gulped. "When we got back from the doctor's, you looked completely terrified."

"I know. And I know that's why you kissed me, because you felt sorry for me, but I've come to terms with it now. The pregnancy. Trent leaving. Being alone. And I'm good."

He did not kiss her out of pity. Why the heck would she ever think that? He stood there, stuffed his hands in his pockets, and something happened in her eyes. They searched his own, as if seeking something. Whatever it was, she must not have found it because her lids lowered and she stepped back from the door and he had a feeling she was disappointed in him somehow.

"Come on in."

Ornaments hung from strings strung across the room. That was what he'd been hearing. The glass balls clinking together as she jumped. She'd doused the clear glass with blue and silver glitter, but from the inside somehow, and there were dozens of them, and even more on the kitchen table, where she'd clearly been in the middle of making them before she'd been carried away by the beat.

"It's for a wedding next month," she said. "We have this whole Disney-movie theme going and we're going to string them up everywhere. I have hundreds of these babies to make, and let me tell you, when I die, they'll still find glitter on my body."

He just shook his head. It was what she did to him that always took him by surprise. She made him smile. Always. Even on that first day he'd met her when she'd been crying her eyes out, she'd made him want to laugh.

"How was the horse show?" she asked, shoving aside some boxes full of ornaments on her kitchen table and inviting him to sit. "You want anything to drink?"

A shot of whiskey.

"It was good." He took a seat. "The horse I rode won some points, not enough to qualify for the world show just yet, but we'll get there."

"Wow. You're going to compete against people from around the world?"

He shrugged. "That's the plan. It was my dad's idea. He's trying to increase the marketability of our stallion, Markie."

"Markie?" She lifted a brow, amusement flashing through her eyes.

"It's a nickname. His real name is GR Make My Mark, and we hope he lives up to his name. He's an amazing horse. Very charismatic. I'll introduce you one day."

"That'd be neat. And I'd like to watch you compete one day, too."

Why did the idea send a shot of adrenaline through him? What would it matter if she watched him ride Markie? Why did it matter so much to him that she was interested in what he did for a living?

"Sure. I have another horse show in a few weeks. It's down south. You could drive down for a day and watch."

She smiled. "I'd like that."

He sat there, looking anywhere but at her, suddenly uncomfortable and on edge and as breathless as a teenage boy on his first date.

He shot up out of his chair. "Well, I just wanted to say thanks for leaving me that lasagna. It was great."

She stayed seated, and there it was in her eyes again, the searching. She was waiting for something from him, something he couldn't give her, because no matter what she'd said in her note, there was no forgetting that kiss and how it'd made him feel. How it'd made them *both* feel, he suspected.

He headed for the door, but she caught his hand as he slipped past her.

"Flynn."

Her eyes were huge, her hand warm, the fingers gently squeezing his own. This was what she'd been searching for, some kind of sign that everything was okay between them.

"We can't," he said.

"I know," she said softly.

"But if you knew how tempted—"

Her pupils flared and it was his turn to wait, to see what she would do next, because his willpower faded with every second. He wanted to pull her up against him, to pick up where they'd left off the other day, but he couldn't…wouldn't.

"You're right." She looked down at her lap. "It would be a huge mistake. I'm pregnant and not thinking clearly and you're off living your life showing horses and taking care of the ranch and I don't want to lose your friendship," she said, a wry smile tipping up one corner of her mouth. "You're kind of the only family I have right now."

Family. That was a good way to think of her.

She let go of his hand, and it was like someone let the air out of his lungs. He couldn't breathe. His hand dropped back to his side, but his fingers flexed thanks to the burn of her touch, and he knew he had it bad. That he wanted Amy in a way he'd never wanted a woman in his life, but she carried another man's child and he just couldn't wrap his head around that.

"I talked to my sister and Charlotte and everybody about throwing you a baby shower," he said, desperate to say something, anything to change the subject. "They said they'd be happy to do it for you."

"What?"

He ducked his head, wondering if he'd overstepped somehow. "When I realized how alone you were, it just sort of made sense. Someone has to do it, and since your mom lives in Florida…"

"You didn't have to do that."

"I know, but I wanted to." He took a deep breath, trying to regain his composure. "You don't have anyone, Amy, and I can't imagine all the things you probably need to do and what you'll need to buy and all the planning that comes along with having a baby. My sister-in-law Ava understands. And so does Jayden. And Charlotte just wants to help. They'll all love it."

"But doesn't Jayden live out of state?"

"They just bought a house down the road from here. She wanted to be closer to home when the baby comes."

"Oh, but then she probably has way too much to do. I couldn't impose. And Charlotte works so hard. No. I can't let them do this for me."

"Are you kidding? Jayden has movers and people to unpack for her and some kind of concierge cleaning service. She was telling me about it the other day. Said it took the fun out of moving, if moving can be considered fun. And Charlotte is so happy with everything you've done for her. She said she'd love to help you out. Kait, my other sister-in-law, wants to help, too, but from a distance."

"They don't have to do that."

"But they want to."

She looked away from him. Was she crying? He couldn't be sure because she wouldn't let him see.

"Will you let them do it?"

He saw her shoulders lift as she took a deep breath, but she nodded, still not looking at him.

"Good."

He wanted to touch her. To soothe her by stroking her cheek with his thumb. Instead, he said, "I should get going."

She nodded again. "Thanks for coming by."

At last she met his gaze and he saw pain in her eyes and resignation and sadness and so many other emotions it would be impossible to put a name to them all.

"I'll see you around."

She lifted her chin. "See you."

He had to leave. Staring into her eyes, at the sadness there, it was his one weakness, the one thing that made him want to do things he shouldn't want to do,. The sadness and the pain. The realization that she was all alone with nobody to lean on and it broke his heart. So he left her, but it was, hands down, one of the hardest things he'd ever had to do.

Chapter 12

Just call her. Just call her. Just call her.

But Amy stared at her phone for a full five minutes before actually picking up the thing and dialing the familiar number. She half hoped her mom wouldn't answer, but like so many times in her life, her mom was doomed to disappoint.

"Hello?"

"Oh, hey, Mom. It's me, Amy."

"I know who it is," said a voice tinged with amusement, although, as always, the words were tinged with a hint of impatience, too. That was always how Amy felt around her mom, as if she were in intrusion into her life.

"Am I interrupting something?" Amy asked.

"It's Monday, honey. What do I always watch on Monday?"

And what was the other thing her mom did? Make her feel stupid.

"I know, I know," she said. "But I have some news that's kind of important?"

"Oh?" But her mom sounded distracted and the television still played in the background and suddenly the speech she'd prepared went out the window.

"I'm pregnant."

Silence. Amy couldn't figure out if it was because her mom was so deeply engrossed in her reality television show that she didn't hear or if she'd shocked her into silence.

"Pregnant?" her mom asked, the word almost a squeak.

Okay, so not distracted any longer. "Yup." She forced a smile, goodness knows why. It wasn't like her mom could see her. "You're gonna be a grandma."

"You've *got* to be kidding me."

That was a little more on par with what Amy had expected. "Nope. Went to the doctor the other day and I am definitely pregnant."

She could hear a rush of air and Amy wondered if her mom was back to smoking again. She could just picture her lighting up. The narrowing of her blue eyes, the wrinkles around her mouth. Smoking had left lines on her mom's face that made her look older than she actually was. Oh, she tried to hide it by bleaching her hair and tanning her face, but some things just couldn't be hidden.

"You going to get rid of it?"

That was also her mom. Always a fount of warmth and empathy. "No, Mom. I told you. You're going to be a grandma." So maybe she hadn't been listening.

"And the father? What does he think?"

That was the one question that made Amy squirm. "He's sort of out of the picture."

More silence. Amy felt herself squirming even with her mom hundreds of miles away.

"What happened?"

"It's a long story."

She couldn't stomach the idea of telling her mom about Trent and Tiffany, but she still felt the sting of embarrassment. She'd worked her tail end off to get to where she was, to make her mom proud, but the truth was she would never measure up. And it hurt.

"So you're going to keep it even though the father's out of the picture?"

"Yup."

"Dear God, why? Who's going to want a woman with a baby on her hip?"

"Why didn't you get rid of me?"

She'd always wanted to ask the question, had never had the nerve before now. If her mom was so miserable raising her, if she'd been so happy to cast her off and move to Florida, why had she had her in the first place?

"Honey, back then we didn't have pills and things like that. It wasn't easy to terminate a pregnancy. These days it's a piece of cake."

Amy's fingers clutched the phone, trying not to let the words hurt her because it was impossible not to interpret her mother's words as confirmation of what she'd always suspected. She really hadn't wanted to have her. If it'd been "easier" to terminate her pregnancy, she would have.

"I'm not getting rid of it, Mom. I'm having a baby. I thought you should know."

"Well, that's unfortunate," her mom said. "But you can still go after him for money and stuff."

Amy just shook her head. "I'll keep you posted on a delivery date. Goodbye, Mom."

"Wait, don't hang up."

Amy waited, her hand tightening even more. What new arrow would her mom sling her way?

"Are you happy about this, Amy?"

She relaxed. "Yes, Mom. I'm happy."

Scared to death. Freaking out inside. Wishing I had a mom who would hold my hand through the whole process. Who might even offer to move in with me to help out.

But Amy knew that would never happen.

"I'll call you later."

"Okay, dear." The volume went up in the background and Amy knew that was it. She'd broken the news. Message received by her mom. It was back to her regularly scheduled programing for Susan Jensen.

Amy hung up, but not before letting out a curse and vowing once again to never, ever be like her mom. Never.

"I know I told Flynn I didn't mind you throwing me a baby shower, but we really don't need a planning party," Amy told Charlotte three days later. "We can do everything via email. No need to meet face-to-face."

Her new friend just shook her head. Light from the kitchen window behind her lit up a face that seemed tinged with exasperation, not surprising since they'd been going back and forth on the baby shower issue for the better part of the last five minutes. And before that, she'd picked Charlotte's brain about paternity suits. Not that she wanted Trent's money, or even his help, but after her conversation with her mom she figured she better have some answers because she knew her mom would ask if she'd explored the issue. Charlotte had been a wealth of knowledge thanks to her job at Child

Protective Services, but she'd insisted she act sooner rather than later where Trent was concerned. For some reason, Amy didn't want to do that and she could tell she'd frustrated Charlotte with her reluctance. And now this. The baby shower.

"Of course you can, Amy. You've done so much for me. This is my way of giving back. Mine and Jayden's and Ava's…all of ours. Well, except for Kait. She's hard to pin down. But she promised she'll come to the baby shower. This would just be dinner. A simple girls' night get-together. Maverick's going to take Olivia up to his dad's house for dinner, so it'll just be the four of us." She nudged her forearm. "Come on. It'll be fun. When was the last time you had a girls' night?"

Never. Not once.

"It's been a while."

"See?" She wiggled in her seat. "Please?"

Amy didn't know what to say. Charlotte had been so kind to her the last few times they'd met, always praising her ideas and telling her what a genius she was. It didn't matter if Amy didn't really believe it—there were wedding planners who were way more brilliant than she was—but it was kind of Charlotte. But this— offering to have a girls' night while they discussed the baby shower Charlotte and Jayden and Ava insisted on throwing her? Well, this was just super nice.

"But Jayden has so much to do. I know Flynn said she had people to handle it all, but they can't do everything for her."

"No, they really can," Charlotte said, eyes filling with amusement. "And you should see the house they bought right down the road. It's ah-mazing. In fact, we're thinking of holding the baby shower there. It's about three times the size of this place."

Three times? She stared out toward the family room, where Olivia played with a toy stable and some horses. Her place would fit in Charlotte's family room, she realized, not that she was complaining. She was just happy to have a roof over her head. Speaking of that...

"Thank you for referring Rachelle to me," she said, hoping to change the subject. "I can't wait to get started on her wedding."

"Rachelle is a doll. I've been working with her for years. You'll love her. And don't change the subject. You're coming over here next weekend to discuss your baby shower. It's my turn to do for *you* what you've done for me." She pointed the pen at her, the one she'd been using to jot down notes. "There. I've decided. You're coming over for dinner next Friday."

Amy was out of arguments, but the whole time she talked to Charlotte about which vendors she recommended for her wedding, she kept wondering why it was so hard for her to accept charity. She supposed it had something to do with her upbringing and her mom always making a big deal out of spending money on her. It didn't matter if it was tennis shoes or a new backpack, her mom always complained, and so she'd learned to do without. Look at her pregnancy, for example. She'd spoken to her mom once since that initial conversation, and not a single offer of help. Not that she wanted any, but wasn't it a mom's place to at least make an offer? Especially since her mom knew Trent was out of the picture? But whatever. It felt strange to have people want to help her, people who didn't expect anything in return.

So that next Friday she showed up, the sound of music penetrating the cool night air. Thanksgiving was right around the corner. They would blink and it would be Christmas, and after that, Charlotte's wedding and after that...

She rested a hand against her belly.

You and me, kid.

"Here she is," Charlotte said the moment she swung open the door. "My lifesaver and the best wedding planner ever."

"No, I'm not," Amy said, peeking around at the other two ladies sitting in the family room. Jayden came forward with what looked like a glass of champagne.

"Sparkling apple juice," she said, her pretty blue eyes alight with friendliness, black hair pulled back in a ponytail. "Although Ava said a new study suggests an occasional glass of wine won't hurt baby, and she should know since she's a doctor, but still. She said better safe than sorry."

"Well, I didn't say it exactly like that," said the one woman in the room Charlotte hadn't met yet. "Hi. I'm Ava."

With her dark hair pulled back, she looked too young to be a doctor, Amy thought, but the smile she gave her was just as friendly as Jayden's and Charlotte's, and Amy admitted this wouldn't be too bad. She didn't have any real friends—she'd been too busy making something of her life—but she liked Charlotte and appreciated how she wanted to help.

"So," Ava said, "Flynn tells us you have nobody to throw you a baby shower."

"Well, I mean, I have a mom, but she lives in Florida."

And she really didn't want to talk to her again. She just couldn't drum up the energy to deal with the emotional fallout of her mom's disappointment. Again. Call her weak, call her a chicken, but she just couldn't do it.

"So that's why we want to have one for you," said

Jayden, and Amy wasn't too proud to admit she hoped she looked as lovely as Jayden did when she was six months along. Actually, they were all gorgeous. Amy felt like the ugly duckling of the group.

"We're going to take care of everything," added Ava with a wide smile.

"It'll be fun," said Charlotte.

Amy took a deep breath. "Okay."

They pulled out pads of paper and pencils and asked her a million questions. She didn't know the sex of the baby. She didn't care what kind of food they served. She needed pretty much everything. She had no clue whom to invite, although Charlotte suggested inviting a few of the brides she'd helped over the years. They discussed where to have it and Jayden suggested her place since Amy's place was so small. Amy mentioned wanting to paint her place, anyway, and Jayden jumped on her words, saying they could all help when the time came. On and on it went and the women across from her were so kind and sweet that near the end of their questioning Amy had the weirdest sensation flow through her. It took her a moment to realize what it was. Gratitude. Joy. Humility. So many emotions she couldn't just pinpoint one.

When they were done, it was all she could do to softly say, "Thank you."

They all three nodded and smiled. Amy wondered if it were possible to adopt all of them. Half sister. Aunt. Cousin. She didn't care.

"But we're not through," Ava said. "Flynn said you've been working your tail off and so we thought we'd have a little fun tonight, too."

"I know how exhausting it is to be pregnant and work," Jayden said, patting her belly.

They all exchanged secret smiles and Amy wondered

what they had up their sleeves. Whatever it was, they couldn't wait to share the idea.

"We're having a pampering pregnant party," Charlotte said. "Jayden spent a small fortune at the beauty store today. You wouldn't believe everything she bought. And, frankly, it's not just you pregnant ladies who need a little R & R."

Charlotte dashed off. She came back with a basket of goodies that had clearly been stashed away earlier. Masks. Scrubs. Even a cucumber or two.

"You don't have to do this for me," Amy said.

"Are you kidding?" Jayden said. "I'd be disappointed if we didn't."

She'd never been invited to do something like this in her life. Never. She just didn't make friends easily. Women her age seemed interested in different things than her, like men and parties and posting selfies. That had never been her. She preferred to throw her energy into the weddings she planned. Social life? Who needed one of those? That was why Trent had seemed too perfect. He'd been happy to let her do her thing while he went off and did his own thing.

Like Tiffany.

"Please stay," Jayden added.

The words were so heartfelt Amy found herself looking away. "Okay." Because the truth was, she felt pretty dumpy and ugly these days. Maybe a little pampering would help her self-esteem.

"Goody," Jayden said.

"Don't feel bad," Ava whispered. "I've never done anything like this, either."

Amy met her new friends' gazes and smiled. Jayden, especially, seemed so poised and confident that it seemed hard to believe she didn't have a weekly spa session. But she supposed things always looked different from the outside looking in.

"I just wish my daughter was here," Ava added. "She'd love this."

"You have a daughter?"

"I do. And a baby boy. So between work and the kids, it's been a long time since I've had girl time."

Ten minutes later they all had masks on their faces and were lounging in the family room, Amy doing her best to share a funny story about a zoologist she'd had as a bride and a monkey that'd run rampant through her wedding guests, although it had gotten harder and harder to talk thanks to a drying mask.

"You mean the monkey stole the woman's purse?" Ava asked.

"It did. Just took off with it, although to be honest it was my bride's fault. I warned her that the little wretch was not to be trusted. You should have seen what it tried to do to the wedding cake, but she insisted her coworker, as she called him, be included in her wedding. We had this whole zoo theme going on. Not terribly clever or original, but that was one of my first weddings to plan, and the bride insisted—"

The door opened and they all three froze, and to her absolute and complete horror, Flynn walked in, took two steps, and stopped dead in his tracks.

"I love the way you just walk in," his sister, Jayden, chastised.

"I've been knocking," he said, "but you clearly couldn't hear me over the sound of the music and your laughing."

Flynn is here.

Her whole body just sort of went oomph, especially

when his gaze met her own, although how he recognized her with all the goo she had on her face, she had no idea.

"Oh, my goodness," Charlotte said. "I forgot you were coming by tonight." She slapped her forehead, then immediately realized she shouldn't have, pulling her hand away and frowning at her palm. She had a bald spot where she'd inadvertently wiped away the green mask. "Let me go get those registration papers for you."

She shot up off the couch.

"So, how are you, big brother?" Jayden said, standing up.

"Oh, no." He waved his hands. "Don't you dare come near me."

"Why ever not?" Jayden asked in a Southern-belle voice, but she stopped. "You sure you don't want to join us? We have extra masks in the basket."

Flynn tipped back his cowboy hat. "Uh, no thanks. I'm not into looking like a leprechaun."

His gaze met her own again and she felt compelled to say, "Hey, Flynn."

"Hey, Amy."

And then Charlotte came bursting back into the room. "I think this is it." She handed Flynn a piece of paper. "I don't pay attention to horse stuff, but the picture matches the horse he's selling."

"These are them," Flynn said. "Thanks."

"While you're here," Jayden said. "Amy was just saying she wanted to do some upgrades to her place. I mentioned having some leftover paint, and since I know you're coming over later this week, maybe you can pick it up and drop it off for her?"

"Oh, no. He doesn't have to do that." Amy's whole body tensed at the thought of Flynn coming by. He'd been keeping his distance lately, sending her text messages, and she didn't blame him; she really didn't. She was so ashamed of her behavior. What kind of woman kissed a man when she was knocked up with another man's baby? She'd turned into some kind of hormonal harlot.

"Flynn doesn't mind," Jayden said. "Do you?"

Flynn had been put on the spot, and he very clearly didn't know what to say. Actually, Amy could tell he wanted to say no, but he didn't.

"I can do that," he said.

"Perfect," Jayden said, and despite her brother's protests, walked up to him and planted a kiss on his chin. "You're just the man for the job."

"Great, now I have gunk on my face," he said, pulling away.

But he didn't wiggle out of getting the paint. Instead he started backing out of the room. "Tell Maverick I'll list Blondie for sale by tomorrow." And with a wave of the paper in his hand, he turned.

"He really doesn't have to grab that paint for me," Amy said.

"Nonsense," Jayden said. "He's always running by the house. It'll be easy."

"But I don't even know if I'll be allowed to paint."

"My dad won't mind. I'll see to that." She smiled. "Now, let's get this stuff off our faces, shall we, ladies? I don't know about you, but I'm starting to crack like an egg."

They all stood up and Amy glanced outside right as Flynn hightailed it out the front door. She wondered if he could see her from the driveway, and if she was the reason he'd left so quickly.

Chapter 13

He sat in the driver's seat for a moment to catch his breath.

What the heck was it about her? Even with her face stained green he couldn't seem to take his eyes off her. It made no sense.

But as he backed out of his brother's driveway, he kept waiting for her to reappear in the window, and when she didn't, he pointed his tires down the road, gunning the engine to the point that he could hear rocks pinging off the undercarriage of his truck.

"Stupid, dumb, ridiculous—"

The list of words he called himself was long, but even as he drove up to his place—the old bunkhouse he used to share with his brothers—he knew he'd have to face facts. For whatever reason, he couldn't stop thinking about her.

Later that week he headed over to her place with a

load of paint cans in the back of his truck. His palms began to sweat as he got closer.

Just get in and out, he told himself. That was all there was to it.

Another truck sat in her driveway, and as ridiculous as it seemed, his first instinct was to slam on the brakes and turn around. But the knee-jerk reaction made no sense. He had no idea if the truck belonged to a man or a woman.

Except it looked like a man's truck.

The hunting stickers on the back window. The massive tires. The shiny rims. Man with a huge ego, one who wanted to make a statement with his vehicle. *Look at me. Here I am. My truck is bigger than yours.*

He didn't stop in her driveway—that would block whoever it was in—so he pulled past the entrance, parking on the road, and the moment he slipped out of the vehicle, he could hear it. Raised voices. Scratch that. One raised voice. A man's.

"You'll have to prove it's mine," the man all but screamed. "Because I don't believe for a minute you're carrying my child."

"Trent," he heard Amy say. "I have no reason to lie—"

"We weren't even having sex. I was seeing Tiffany and trying to break things off with you."

"We had sex. Do you remember that night you came home drunk and I had to put you to bed and you pulled me down."

"That wasn't sex. That was just some groping and kissing."

"It was sex."

"Not that I remember."

"I'm not having this conversation with you, Trent. The baby is yours whether you believe me or not."

Flynn stood outside the house, trying to decide if he should stay or go. Probably go. But just as he was about to turn, the front door swung open and he came face-to-face with a dark-haired man with narrow shoulders and painted-on blue jeans.

"Who's this?"

Amy appeared behind him, and there was no mistaking the surprise he spotted in her eyes, nor the instant flash of humiliation.

"That's Flynn Gillian, the landlord's son."

"What's he doing here?"

"I'm dropping off paint." Any thought of leaving fled the moment Flynn spotted the anguish in Amy's eyes. "Amy wants to paint before the baby arrives."

"Hell, Amy, for all I know he could be the father," Trent said, pointing with his thumb in his direction.

"I told you, take a DNA test."

Flynn could hear the frustration in her voice.

"That's all you have to do to prove it once and for all."

"Nope. This isn't my problem." Trent glanced back at him. "I only came over here today to tell you to leave me alone, and leave Tiffany alone, too. You had no business trying to contact her."

"You're right. I shouldn't have done that, but I was desperate to get your attention."

"Well, you got it. Leave us alone, Amy. Move on with your life. If you're really pregnant, the baby should be your primary focus now."

"If I'm really *pregnant*?"

"I've got to go." Trent turned.

Flynn blocked his path. "She really is pregnant."

The man was shorter than he was, with eyes that

were set too close together and a pointy chin. Flynn had no idea what she'd ever seen in him.

"How do you know that?"

"Because I was at her first doctor's appointment with her. I saw it up on the screen. She's pregnant."

Trent glanced back at Amy before meeting his gaze again. "You went to the doctor's office with her?"

"Because she had no one else," Flynn said. "Because you'd abandoned her, and she was alone and scared and had nobody to turn to."

"I'm out of here."

Trent tried to walk around him, but Flynn blocked his path again. He was tempted to grab the man by the shoulders but changed his mind.

"You are the baby's father, whether you want to believe it or not, and the sooner you realize that, the easier this will be on everyone. Amy's done nothing wrong. Her only fault was thinking you were man enough to accept the truth, but clearly that isn't the case. But you better get used to the idea of being a father, and you better tell your new girlfriend about your impending fatherhood, too, because once the baby comes there'll be no denying a DNA test." He leaned in closer. "None."

The man stared up at him and Flynn could see his words were finally beginning to sink in. Trent's Adam's apple bobbed up and down as he swallowed the bitter truth.

"Go home. Think about what I'm trying to tell you, and when you come to your senses, get in touch with Amy. She'll need your help with the child."

He stepped out of the man's way. Trent all but ran to his truck, climbing inside and starting the engine and driving away without looking at either of them in the process.

"Thank you."

The words were full of heartfelt sincerity, Flynn glancing down at Amy, who'd come up alongside him.

"I had no idea he was going to show up here, but I guess calling his girlfriend at work finally got his attention."

"You did what?"

She shot him a look of sheepish regret and turned back to the little house. He followed her inside.

"I was desperate. And after talking to your sister, I thought I should at least try and see him face-to-face before slapping him with a paternity suit, which is what it sounds like I'm going to have to do, anyway."

The realization clearly upset her. She didn't like confrontation. He didn't blame her. He hated it, too.

"And to think, I thought once I told him the baby's sex, he'd be happy."

"You know what you're having?"

She turned to her tiny kitchen table, picking up a piece of paper. "While you were gone I had my blood work done, including a genetic test that can determine the sex of the baby." She handed him the paper. He scanned it, but she said, "I'm having a girl," before he could finish reading it.

He handed the paper back to her. "Congratulations."

"You think?" she asked, going to the table and dropping the paper at the same time she sank into one of the chairs. "Because I don't know, Flynn. My mom tells everyone she knows that having a girl is a major pain in the rear."

"This is the same mom who moved away without telling you."

"One and the same."

"Then I don't know how much stock I'd put into what

she says. I happen to have some experience with baby girls and they're adorable."

"Until their teenage years. That's what my mom always said."

And suddenly she looked so despondent and demoralized and just plain exhausted that he found himself moving toward her. He debated with himself for a full five seconds before he gave in to the urge that so frequently came over him whenever she was near. He touched her cheek.

"It'll be okay."

She looked up at him with big puppy-dog eyes and said, "That's what you keep saying."

"It will."

At least he didn't want to kiss her this time. All he wanted to do was pull her into his arms and hold her, another urge that happened a lot whenever she was near.

"If it makes you feel any better, I happen to have some pink paint in the back of my truck."

"You do?"

"Jayden used it in Paisley's room, but she bought too much so I have two unopened cans."

"Oh, perfect."

"And if you like, I'll even help you paint."

Those eyes of hers. They were killing him.

"You don't have to do that." She shook her head. "I've imposed enough already."

She didn't look all that enthusiastic and he realized she'd sunk into a funk. He hated that the dancing, bouncing mom-to-be seemed so bummed out today. But could he blame her? She'd just been face-to-face with her ex and he'd called her a liar and told her to stay away from him.

"I didn't even have time to show him the sonogram."

He stood there feeling useless and terrible and anxious all at once. What were these strange feelings she aroused in him?

"I doubt he'd care about seeing his unborn child."

Her lower lip began to tremble. "No," she said softly. "You're probably right."

To hell with it. He pulled her up against him. She sank into his arms as if it was the most natural thing in the world to do. Her own hands slipped beneath his elbows, around the back of him, holding on to him as if her life depended on it.

"I guess I just had this fantasy that he'd show up here and look at the paperwork and—I don't know— tell me he was sorry and ask what he could do to help," she said, her words muffled from pressing her cheek against his chest.

"Amy, I think it's time to realize he's never going to do that. Maybe with time, and after a court-ordered paternity test, but not before the baby comes. Not without a minor miracle."

She nodded, her nose pressing into his chest, and he wondered if she was crying, but he didn't want to look, because if he did, if he spotted tearstained cheeks, he might do something ridiculous again, or worse, something wholly inappropriate given the circumstances.

"Miracles are pretty rare in my life."

His life, too. But as he thought about it, he realized that was totally wrong. A few years ago, he would have sworn his dad would remain a stubborn, cranky old bastard, and yet he'd changed. And he never would have thought Reese Gillian would forgive his sister for getting knocked up at such a young age, but he had. And then there was Olivia, his brother's little girl, the one Charlotte had brought into their life. If ever there was a miracle it was that little girl and what she'd survived and how lucky she'd been to be adopted by his brother and to have someone like Charlotte as her future mother. No. The Gillian family had been blessed in many ways. Yes, there'd been tragedy, but they'd overcome it all just like Amy would. He supposed that was why he wanted to help her so badly. He was just paying it forward.

"Look. We're going to pick a color and paint your room today. I'll drive back to the ranch and get some more supplies. You hang tight."

He did it then; he drew back and met her gaze. Just as he feared, her eyes were rimmed with red. But she wiped at her cheeks, squared her shoulders, and he wanted to say, "Attagirl."

"Are you sure? Do you really have time for that?"

No. He had ten horses to ride, and just as many stalls to muck. He had phone calls to return and paperwork to do.

"I'm sure."

Because to hell with it. Some things were more important than working all the time.

Chapter 14

They painted.

True to his word, he rode off into the sunset and returned with a saddlebag full of paint. Okay, not really. But Jayden hadn't been kidding when she'd said she had a lot of leftovers.

"We could paint St. Paul's Cathedral with all this latex," she told Flynn as she stared into the bed of his truck.

"I know. I'm thinking I might snag any leftovers for my own place."

"There will probably be lots of leftovers. I don't plan on using much. But I'll take that maroon and the green and the white."

"Not the pink?"

She shook her head.

He shot her a look. "You planning on painting an Italian flag on your wall?"

His words almost made her laugh. "No. Something

better. But it's going to take some time, and you won't be able to help me with the final product, but I still need to paint the base color. That light blue will work. Let's get started on that. I moved all the furniture out of the way while you were gone."

So they got to work and the whole time they did, Amy thought about Trent, and the more she thought about him, the harder she rolled the blue paint up and down the wall.

"Whoa," Flynn said, smiling. "You're flicking paint all over the place."

"I know. I'm sorry," she said, wiping at a splotch on her face and probably making a bigger mess of herself. Thankfully, she'd changed into an old T-shirt and jeans and thrown a scarf over her head. "I'm just tired of letting Trent push me around. It's time to take action. If he won't admit to being the baby's father, he can deal with the Department of Child Support Services from here on out."

"Good for you."

She went back to painting, thinking she really didn't deserve a friend like him. Or maybe she did. After all she'd been through, maybe Flynn was God's way of saying "I've been a jerk. Here's a bone." Either way, she appreciated Flynn. With any luck, one day soon she'd forget what it was like to be kissed by a man like him because as she worked alongside him in the tiny little room, the smell of paint barely masking his masculine scent, she grew more and more aware of the fact that they were in a bedroom. But at the same time, it seemed wrong of her to have those kinds of thoughts. The last thing she should be thinking about was another man.

They finished in record time, and Amy and Flynn stood back to admire their handiwork.

"You have paint all over your face," Flynn said.

"I know," she said. "I'm going to need to take a shower."

And suddenly, just like that—*boom*—a change in the air, one that made their gazes connect, and she knew what he was thinking.

Naked bodies. Warm water. Soap.

She was thinking the same thing, except he couldn't possibly be thinking about doing that with *her*. He was just probably thinking about doing that with someone else. Someone skinny with blond hair and blue eyes.

"I'm going to go rinse off my paint roller outside."

Fresh air. That was what she needed. Oxygen to restore her sanity because she could have sworn she'd seen something in his eyes, something that made her grow still, but also quaky and afraid and yet brave all at the same time because she didn't move. She stood there, daring him maybe.

To do *what*?

Kiss her, a little voice answered. She wanted him to kiss her and to help her live out every fantasy she'd ever had about him because there'd been some doozies in recent weeks. But every time her fantasy would get rolling, she'd hear her mom's voice in her head.

No man will want a woman with a child.

The words were practically the first thing her mom had said when she'd called to tell her she was pregnant. They always stopped her fantasies cold, that and…

He could do so much better than her. The man could have practically anyone. Her own doctor had the hots for him. What in heaven's name could he ever see in someone like her? Someone who was so uninteresting her own mother had moved across the country just to get away from her. Someone who'd been looking for love her whole life, but who couldn't seem to find it.

But he didn't look turned off by her. His expression was gentle as he stared down at her.

"Amy," he said softly.

Her name coming off his lips did something to her insides, something that left in its wake ripples of good old-fashioned desire.

"Yes?" she said, because she didn't know what else to do. There was a look in his eyes, one that made her think maybe her fantasies weren't so one-sided after all.

"I'd like to kiss you."

Oh, yes. Please.

She didn't know how it happened, but one minute she was holding a paint roller, and the next he was moving toward her, slowly bending and then—oh, heavens—kissing her again. His lips were warm, and he smelled faintly of paint, and his big hands were at her hips and she wondered if he could feel how fat she'd gotten. That was her last coherent thought because he pressured her to open her mouth and she did exactly that and when his tongue slipped inside and she tasted Flynn, *really* tasted him, the sweetness of his mouth was something she didn't think she could ever get enough of—she was lost.

His hands moved up, his thumbs finding the bottoms of her breasts, and he could have been touching her bare flesh given the way her body reacted, but then one of his hands slipped beneath her shirt and he was cupping her and deepening the kiss at the same time and she'd never been more aroused in her life.

He pulled away. She gasped, her lips burning from the pressure of his mouth, her brain starved for oxygen, but he'd only left her so he could bend and—

Oh, heavens.

He kissed the tip of her breast. Gently, the end puckering as if to say "Well, hello there," and her back arched because those same nipples were so dang sensitive that it felt as if his kiss touched every nerve ending in her body.

He took the hint, his mouth capturing the end, suckling her, and she groaned. Her knees lost the ability to support her. He must have realized she was putty— like, literally, a soft puddle of goo in his hands because he backed her up a step, laid her down on the bed, but he had to break contact with her breast to do so, and it brought her back to reality with a thump.

What could he possibly see in her? she thought again.

He stood above her, a fantasy come to life, Flynn Gillian with his dark hair and dark brows and blue, blue eyes, and she wondered, now that he was staring down at her, if he'd change his mind. If he'd see the same thing she saw when she looked in the mirror. A slightly pudgy, not very pretty, soon to be hugely pregnant woman.

"You're so beautiful."

She stopped breathing for a moment, something inside her tightening and tightening as she looked into his eyes, something that made her eyes fill with tears.

"I'm not, especially not now. I used to be skinny, but I'm not anymore—"

"Shh." He tossed his cowboy hat off to the side. "Just shh."

He was bending again and it felt like a five-alarm fire, and it was such a crazy way to feel, but the heat only tripled when he didn't lie down next to her. Instead, he kneeled, lifting her shirt, pulling it and the scarf on her head off her body.

"I have paint all over my face," she said.

"You look adorable."

She didn't, couldn't. She probably had paint in places she couldn't even see, but then he was pulling her bra down and she knew he was going to do that thing to her breast again, and inside her head the word *wahoo* rang out, but then he was slowly bending toward her. Teasing. He was taking his time on purpose, and her nipple responded instantly, both of them did, puckering.

She really had nice-sized breasts now.

His tongue circled the tip. She about came off the bed. Oh, lordy, did he ever do it for her. He knew exactly how to kiss her and how to touch her, his teeth grazing first one nipple and then the next.

"Flynn." She sighed, arching toward him again.

His hand cupped her, his fingers playing with one nipple while his mouth worked the other, and if she'd thought it'd been a five-alarm fire before, it was a damn forest fire now. She began to pant because it was a form of torture, this kissing her, when she wanted so much more. She wanted it all. She wanted *him*.

She wiggled out from under him, her hands going to the snap of her jeans, but then she froze because if she went through with this, if she allowed him to see her completely naked, he would see it, the baby bump. Small though it might be, it was still there, still a reminder of who she was and what she'd done and that one day soon her belly would be huge and the baby inside wasn't his.

Hands brushed her own. She looked up and met his gaze. He knew what she was thinking, she could tell. He undid her jeans, released the zipper, slid them down over her hips, and there it was. The bulge. The big babypalooza. Her bun in the oven. When she'd first met him, you could barely tell it was there. But in recent weeks her stomach had changed, her belly button beginning to turn inside out, her skin taut. It wasn't very attractive.

He kissed her bump.

She wanted to cry. This man, this amazing man, he didn't care that she was pregnant, or that she'd made mistakes. For some crazy reason he wanted her and, boy howdy, did she ever want him.

A hand grazed her center.

She gasped, closed her eyes. He started working his way up her body, kissing her along the way, and she realized at some point she'd removed her bra, although she didn't even remember doing it, and when his mouth found her breast again, she groaned, because he was touching her down there and kissing her breast at the same time, and it was as if her body had turned into some kind of sexual instrument—one he played so expertly she found herself on the brink of climax in an instant.

"Flynn," she cried out, clutching the sheet she'd thrown over her bed to protect it from paint.

He had to know what he was doing to her, because his mouth found her own and his tongue slipped inside her mouth in the same way he touched her down there, and that was it for her. One tiny little thrust and her hips shot up off the bed and she cried out against his mouth and thought the world might collapse down on her. It didn't, but she fell back to the bed as if it had, at least that was what it felt like. He kept kissing her and nuzzling her the whole time and she realized he'd slipped his arms around her, and that he held her.

"Good?" he asked.

"No, it was terrible."

She heard a low rumble, realized he was laughing. She shifted in his arms, met his gaze for the first time in what seemed like an eternity.

"It's honestly never felt like that before. I wonder if it's the pregnancy. It was…different."

He smiled. "Different is good."

"But...what about you?" she asked.

He smiled, shook his head, and she could see he wasn't the type of man who demanded equal pay for equal services—unlike Trent. Instead, he pulled her close to him again, her ear coming to rest against his chest, his heart beating against his ribs in a comforting rhythm.

"Don't worry about me."

But she did worry about him. She worried about what he would think of her for jumping into bed with him the same day Trent had told her to get lost. She had a habit of doing that. Of getting intimate with men too soon. Would he think she was desperate or something? Maybe she *was* desperate.

"I should get going," he said.

And suddenly, she felt self-conscious, more self-conscious than she'd ever felt in her life, probably because everything about her body seemed bigger, and no matter what he said, there was nothing "adorable" about it.

"I should rinse out the paint rollers." She shuffled to the side, scouting around for her jeans and her T-shirt and hoping like heck he hadn't spotted the cellulite on her thighs. It looked more pronounced in the bright daylight of the room.

"I'll help."

"No, that's okay." She spotted her T-shirt, made a dash for it, never more grateful in her life than when she tugged it on. She spotted her jeans next, one of the denim legs perilously close to the paint tray. She couldn't look at him as she pulled them on. She had no idea where her bra went, but at this point in their relationship, did she really need to worry about covering the girls up? Probably not.

"You sure?" he asked.

"I've taken up enough of your time."

Her cheeks had begun to burn, although she had no idea why, probably because she wished—oh, how she wished—things were different and she wasn't pregnant.

No man will want a woman with a baby on her hip.

Or whatever her mom had said. She tried to get the words out of her mind.

He found his cowboy hat and shoved it on his head. He stood there for a moment, tucking his hands into the pockets of his jeans, and she wanted to look away because her eyes felt suspiciously warm.

"I'm sure," she said, lifting her chin.

She would act like this was no big deal. To heck with her mom. Maybe she was wrong.

"I'll call you later," he said, bending and kissing her on the cheek and just the brush of his lips made her body snap and say "Hello there" again.

But he stepped back.

She watched him walk away, and when she heard the front door close, she sank down on the bed, a hand reaching up to touch her lips.

"Damn you, Mom," she told the room at large.

Chapter 15

He drove back to the ranch like a bat out of hell. Oddly, it was his dad's voice that he heard in his head as he drove along.

Dumb move, son.

And the imaginary father figure in his head was no less censorious than the real-life version. At least they hadn't… Well, they hadn't done…*that.*

But not because he didn't want to. Oh, no. Walking away from her had been nearly impossible to do.

When he pulled up in front of his place, he must have sat in his truck for a good half hour questioning his judgment, wondering how they would move forward, hoping she didn't read more into the situation than there was. But the longer he sat there, the more he couldn't escape one fact: kissing her had been so supremely and utterly perfect it had blown his mind. The way her lips fit his own. The taste of her, like sipping from the blooms of a honeysuckle, something he'd done as a kid. The heat of her and the way her body felt against his own. He could have gone on kissing her and touching her all day, each time she'd opened her mouth to him sending him closer to the brink of…something.

When he got out of his truck, a black-and-white dog got up from her position by his front door.

"Sadie."

His brother's dog lowered her head, tail wagging, her steps quickening as she got closer to him.

"You shouldn't be here. They're going to worry about you."

The dog sat down at his feet and Flynn squatted down and rubbed his fingers through her thick coat. The border collie liked to hang out at his home, Flynn suspected, because she needed a break from the two-year-old tyrant called his niece. Oh, he loved Olivia to pieces, but the little girl liked to pretend Sadie was a horse, climbing on her and "riding" her. The other day, she'd wrapped an electric cord around her as if it was a bridle. Thank God Maverick had caught her, but the poor dog clearly needed some alone time.

"Come down here for some peace and quiet, huh?"

They both went over to the porch, Flynn sitting down. Sadie sat down next to him, the two of them surveying the oaks and the pastures and hills in front of them.

"The thing is she's pregnant," he told the dog. "I mean, what kind of idiot gets involved with a pregnant woman?"

The dog turned to look at him. He rubbed her soft ears.

"I mean, aside from Shane. But that was different. He knocked Kait up. And they got married right after.

This is different. And that asshole who got her pregnant. Trent. What a loser."

She'd looked so miserable after Trent had left. Nobody deserved to be treated that way.

"I guess I'll just have to make it clear we're still just friends."

The dog licked his hand. He didn't know what it was about her soulful brown eyes, but he always felt like she knew exactly what he was saying.

"The thing is, Sadie, I like her way more than a friend."

He refused to complicate her life, though. Hell, getting involved with her would complicate his own damn life. What about his plans to qualify Markie for the world show? He didn't have time to cart Amy around to the doctor or hold her hand through her pregnancy. He wasn't ready to settle down. He had things to do with his life. Having a kid like Shane and Carson and soon Jayden, that wasn't part of the plan. Not for a long while yet, and dating Amy meant taking on a kid.

He didn't call her that night. He chickened out. He sent her a text instead, wishing her good-night and promising to talk to her tomorrow. She replied back instantly.

Ditto.

He stared at the word for a full five seconds.
Ditto?
What the hell did that mean? Would she call him? And why did he feel so let down by her one-word response?

He was still wondering about it the next day. He'd just finished working Markie. The stallion's coat glistened with sweat, and Flynn decided to cool him off by walking along the rail of the arena. He'd only made two laps when he spotted her walking toward him in jeans and a white T-shirt, her hair loose around her shoulders.

"Hi there."

Even from a distance he could see her smile, a hand lifting as she waved energetically. Flynn's stomach did something funny as she came toward him.

"I walked," she announced once she was near enough for him to hear. Across the road, her voice startled some birds from a row of grapevines. "Although, if I'd known how long it would take to get here, I probably wouldn't have done it." She came closer and closer, eventually stopping near the rail, cheeks flushed from being out of doors. He pulled up Markie. There were no clouds in the sky, but there was still a chill in the air, a slight breeze blowing and pulling the shirt tight across her abdomen and the small bulge of her pregnancy.

He'd kissed that belly yesterday.

"I kept following the trail you left behind the other day," she said. "And it was like one of those dreams. You know, the one where you're trying to find your way home, only you can't. I kept thinking this place would be over the next hill, or around the next bend in the road, only it wasn't. What are you? Fifty miles away from my place?"

"I don't know," he said. "I don't think we've ever measured it."

"Well, I'm here to tell you, that horse you rode over the other day is probably sore. I know I'm going to be. My goodness."

She smiled, and it was as if nothing had happened. At least, that was what she was aiming for, but she couldn't quite carry it off because there was tension in her shoulders and worry in her eyes.

"Who's this?" she asked brightly, too brightly.

"Markie."

Her brows lifted. "Ah," she said. "The pride and joy of Gillian Ranch."

But she didn't try to approach him and that was probably just as well. Markie was a good boy, but he was still a stallion and you had to watch yourself around them. She didn't move and he didn't say anything, but that was only because he knew she was having a hard time formulating what she'd come here to say.

"Listen, about yesterday," she said at last, but she looked down, dragging her toe through the grass that ringed the arena as if making patterns only she could see. He watched as she took a deep breath, squared her shoulders and met his gaze again. "I hope you don't think—" another breath "—that, you know, I expect anything from you."

She looked uncomfortable and worried and brave all at the same time. "We were just messing around. I get that. It didn't mean anything. I mean, I'm not trying to turn you into some kind of surrogate baby daddy or something." She tried smiling. "I won't be expecting flowers and a sappy card on Valentine's Day or invitations to dinner or anything."

He didn't know what to say. It was like entering a dark room. He was afraid to make a wrong turn. What did she want him to say?

"Anyway, I just came over to tell you that."

"You didn't need to do that."

But hadn't she? Wasn't there just the tiniest part of him that had worried she was looking for a substitute daddy for her kid? The thought shamed him because no matter what his father's voice might say, the one that had cast doubts on her character and reproached him for losing control of his feelings for her yesterday, deep down inside he'd known she wasn't the type to try to seduce him into sticking around or something.

He slipped off Markie, losing sight of her for a moment while he loosened the girth. Markie sighed and dropped his head, and Flynn went around to the other side where he leaned against the rail.

"You coming over for Thanksgiving?" he asked.

Her eyes widened a bit. "Me?"

"Yeah. You should. Whole family will be there."

The change of subject had clearly thrown her. "But don't you think that'd be strange? The wedding planner at Thanksgiving dinner?"

"Not at all."

She frowned and he could tell she fretted over something. It was one of the things he liked about her. She wore her emotions on her sleeve. He could see every thought that crossed into her mind. Right now, she was puzzled and maybe a little bit concerned.

"That's not why I came over, you know. To make you feel guilty or something. You don't have to take pity on me and invite me to a family dinner."

He shook his head. "I don't feel sorry for you at all. You just don't have any family, at least none nearby. You said so yourself. So you should come over. Don't be alone for the holiday."

She didn't just jump at his words. If he'd had any doubt that she was trying to trap him into a relationship or whatever, it was all there in her face. Her reluctance to intrude. A burgeoning hope that she wouldn't have to spend the holidays alone. Her fear that she would be imposing.

"Please."

Hope won out. She smiled. "I'd like that."

"Good."

She stood there. "So we're still friends."

"Friends," he said.

Except he didn't want to be just friends. Not anymore. As he stared down at her, he realized he admired her in a way he'd never admired a woman before.

"I'll see you next week, then."

He nodded, and she smiled, gave a little wave and headed back the way she'd come. He almost called out to her, told her to hold up a second, that he'd give her a ride home, but something held him back, something that had to do with the realization he was getting in too deep, too fast.

It scared him. Scared him a lot.

She felt him watch her as she walked away, but she was proud of herself. She handled herself well, she thought. She could hold her head high. She hadn't come off as needy or clingy, just matter-of-fact.

Friends.

The pride she felt lasted right up until the moment she let herself into her home, and then all of the doubts and insecurities came crashing back, the same ones she always felt when a relationship was new and exciting and she wondered... *Will this one stick around?*

She made a point not to call him that week. She had a tendency to lay it on too thick when a relationship was new. It was a flaw that she wouldn't allow to affect her and Flynn. So she focused on the wedding she had the first week of December, finalizing things with the caterer, checking in with the florist and holding the bride's hand—mostly through telephone conversations and text messages. The theme for the wedding had been the bride's idea. She loved the movie *Frozen*, and Amy had been happy to go along, coming up with unique ways to make the walls of the chapel look like cracked ice. Fake snow, which had meant lining the wooden floors of their venue—an old barn up in the hills—with Visqueen first. Total pain in the rear, but when she'd tested a small section at the bride's house, her client was thrilled. They would even turn down the heat, having warned people to dress warmly. And, of course, there were the glass balls she'd made to hang from the ceiling. Hundreds of them. She couldn't wait to pull it all off, although a part of her was stressed to the max about the whole thing. That always happened the week before a wedding, which was why she was almost glad to have a break.

"You ready to eat some food?" she asked the little girl inside her. "I'm thinking I should walk over again. Goodness knows I'll probably eat enough that they'll have to roll me down their hill."

It had grown cold over the past week. She bundled up as she made her way toward the center of Gillian Ranch. Now that she knew how long the walk would take, perversely, it didn't seem to take as much time. They were eating in the late afternoon and it had dawned a truly spectacular day. The sky was a vivid cerulean blue, the clouds that floated overhead bleached stark white by the sun. On the other side of a rock wall, mares and their foals frolicked in the chilly air. Frost from the morning had left a sheen of dew on the trees and the grass, and the effect was dazzling, dewdrops sparkling, the smell of dank earth filling her with a peace she hadn't felt in a long time.

It would be okay.

Her business was taking off, thanks in large part to Charlotte Bennett. The woman seemed to know half the people in Via Del Caballo and she'd been her biggest advocate. It seemed like every other day her phone rang and someone Charlotte had talked to was on the other end. If this kept up, she'd be completely booked the following year. Her little business might be the success she'd always dreamed of, just in time for the baby.

The trail she'd been following suddenly turned into a gravel road and she knew she was getting close. On the right would be a cabin. Flynn's home, the place where he'd taken her what seemed like a lifetime ago. He was probably up at his dad's house, she thought, expecting to see an empty driveway. Instead, she spotted Flynn's big black truck, and she tensed.

Was he home?

Did she just walk by? Ring the doorbell? Call out "Hello"? She chose the first option, nearly jumping out of her skin when the front door opened.

"Decided to walk?" he asked.

She nodded mutely because she couldn't think—she honestly had a hard time forming words. He stood on his porch in his cowboy hat and jeans, and he looked so gloriously handsome that it was as if time had slowed down and she stood face-to-face with a cowboy of old. His mouth moved, but it took a few seconds for his words to make sense.

"I was mashing up potatoes and saw you from the kitchen window."

Because he cooked. Of course he did. She'd known that. He was also kind to animals and had a penchant for rescuing women in distress.

And she was falling in love with him.

She stood there, staring into his kind blue eyes, and

she knew it just as surely as she knew Trent was the biggest jerk who ever walked the earth. And that what she'd felt toward the men who'd come before Trent was nothing compared to how she felt toward Flynn.

Oh, dear goodness.

"I'll see you up there, then," she called out brightly, waving, because she had to leave. She had to go before he saw something in her eyes, because the dratted man could read her like the Sunday paper and she didn't want him to catch a glimpse of the hero worship in her eyes. That would be terrible and embarrassing and humiliating because she had no business, none, falling in love with a man when she was pregnant with another man's child.

Dear Lord, Amy, are you insane?

"No, don't go," he said.

Nope. Nope. She wasn't going to listen to him.

"You can help me carry my twice-baked potatoes up there. I have two trays and I was planning on driving, but it seems stupid to drive that little way. Hang on. Better yet, come inside. I still have to fill the potato shells and sprinkle cheese on them."

"I can't," she said, but then realized the words sounded crazy because there was no earthly reason why she couldn't help him carry his dang potatoes. It wasn't like he was asking her to carry tubes of viral plague. "I mean, I shouldn't. I'm going to be late."

He took a step toward her. She was like a deer in the forest, the one that spots a human and freezes for a moment right before it bounds off. Except she couldn't dart off. She just stood there staring up at him and thinking he was the kindest, most generous man she'd ever met and she wanted—oh, how she wanted—to go up to him and bury her head in his chest and inhale his scent because he was all the man she'd ever need…and he would never be hers. Never.

"What's wrong?" he asked.

Nope. She would not turn into helpless Amy again. Not now of all times.

"Nothing. I just told Charlotte I'd be up there early, and then I decided to walk and I forgot how long it took to get here…"

She was rambling and Flynn, sharp eared as he always was, had noticed it. He took another step.

"Amy, come inside. I'm not going to kiss you again if that's what you're afraid of."

Was he kidding? That was what she wanted. She wanted his kisses and his touch, but most of all, the haven of his arms.

"I'm sorry I let things get out of hand the other day. I just sort of let you take the fall about how things went too far and that was wrong of me. It's been bugging me for a week now. It wasn't your fault. Not at all. It was my fault."

He thought it was *his* fault? Who was he kidding? She'd practically jumped him.

"You don't have to apologize."

And he was wrong. She wasn't afraid of him wanting to kiss her. She was afraid of herself. Afraid she'd let him see how much she cared for him. Afraid she'd fall even harder if she spent any more time in his company. Afraid of what it would be like to have her baby and watch from a distance as Flynn fell in love with some cute rancher's daughter who knew how to ride and delivered baby cows in her spare time.

"Come on inside," he said again.

She couldn't. She just couldn't. But as if from a distance she heard herself say, "Okay." And then, because she felt really, really stupid for agreeing, added, "But just for a second."

He waited for her and the closer she got, the more aware of him she became. Her superhuman sense of smell caught a whiff of him, all sandalwood and sweat, and she wished for a moment that she had the nerve to take his hand and say, "Forget about Thanksgiving dinner. Let's go to bed instead."

"It's a mess inside," he said. "Been cooking these damn potatoes all day. My oven is so small I've had to do them in batches. Can't wait to build my own home where I'll have counter space galore—oh, and a wall of cabinets and a really big fridge."

"Yeah?"

That was good. Just keep it casual. Act like your ovaries are still working and you haven't lost your mind.

"Yeah. I plan on building a place by the entrance to the ranch, away from where I work. I love where I grew up, but I need something different."

"So do you and your brothers get to pick a place to build or something? Is that how it works?"

"Oh, no," he said, going to the oven and pulling out a sheet of baked potatoes. "My father isn't the type to hand things over to any of his kids. Part of each paycheck goes toward a fund he set up for me. Actually, he set the same thing up for all of us, including Jayden, except she never worked the ranch so it didn't really apply. Anyway, we agreed on a purchase price for the bare land and I get to pay for the rest, and I should be able to do that pretty quickly if I win an open championship on the cutting horse circuit, which I plan to do with Markie. My dad and I own him together, so we get to split his earnings."

He'd told her much the same before, and yet there

was a part of her that hadn't really believed it. She figured there had to be some perks for living and working at the ranch, seeing as it was a family operation, but she guessed not. Well, aside from the unlimited supply of land. And being able to put aside his earnings.

"I even get charged for staying here. Of course, it's not a whole lot, but that's how my dad is. He didn't want to raise a bunch of spoiled, namby-pamby sons—his words—and I think for the most part, we all turned out okay."

You think?

That was what she said inside her head. Better than okay. Every single member of the Gillian family she'd met had been so kind and humble and amazing that it was no wonder she found herself falling for the man. She was falling in love with his family, too.

"Maybe you can start filling the potatoes while I finish mashing this last batch." He pointed to a bowl and the creamy potatoes he'd apparently whipped up inside. "We can cheese them together."

"Yeah, sure," she quipped.

He smiled. Her heart did the cartoon equivalent of jumping out of her chest and landing at his feet. She had to turn away, but her hands shook, she realized.

She was falling for him and it was crazy and stupid and the most ridiculous thing in the world because she was pregnant. Preg-nant. No man in his right mind could look past that, just as her mother had said…not even a man as remarkable as Flynn.

Chapter 16

Something had changed between them, Flynn thought. Something that he wished with all his heart he could get back because no matter what he'd told her, he had to fight an urge to kiss her again. But she could barely look at him and he kept rambling on about growing up on the ranch and his plans for the future and he knew that she knew that no matter what either of them claimed, they could never go back to being "just friends."

"You ready?" he asked once he sprinkled the last of the cheese on two trays of twice-baked potatoes.

"Sure, yeah," she said.

"You want to walk?" He wiped his hands on the front of his pants, not because of the cheese on his fingers, but because his palms were sweating. He needed to get her out of there.

"Yes, actually." He could have sworn he heard her add, "I need air."

He turned back to her sharply, almost tempted to ask her if he'd heard her correctly, but she picked up the tray of potatoes and all but ran from the kitchen, and he knew—he just knew—she felt it, too. The chemistry between them. It was off the charts. He wanted to kiss her again. No, he wanted to do way more than kiss her.

"Amy," he said.

She turned back to him so sharply she damn near made Frisbees out of the potatoes. She caught herself just in time, tipping the tray back, but too quickly, the cheesy potatoes face planting into the fancy Western T-shirt she wore.

And maybe it was the tension in the air. Maybe it was her expression of sheepish embarrassment, but for whatever reason, he started to laugh.

"It's not funny," she said.

"Lean forward," he told her. "I think we can salvage them."

She did as instructed, leaning forward, Flynn taking the tray from her. When she straightened, there were bits of cheese stuck everywhere.

He tried not to laugh.

"I've ruined my shirt."

"No, you haven't. You just need to brush it off."

She looked so crestfallen that he couldn't help himself, he tipped her chin up, and as always happened when he looked into her eyes, he felt something shift inside him, something crazy and remarkable and frightening all at the same time.

"It's okay," he said softly.

She shook her head. "No, it's not."

He ached to hold her. Literally, the muscles in his arms burned.

"This has nothing to do with potatoes, does it?"

She shook her head.

"What is it?"

But he knew. Deep inside, he knew. She suffered from the same overwhelming urge to touch him and hold him and kiss him as he did her.

"I don't know what to do," she admitted, her voice almost a groan.

"I know," he said, the heat in his arms spreading throughout his body.

She peered into his eyes, seeming to look into first one, and then the other, and she said nothing, but he knew she studied him—every line and angle and plane of his face. She memorized him, or so it seemed.

"I want you," she admitted. "I want you so badly it hurts."

Damn her brutal honesty. The words were like a hot poker to his groin.

"I want you, too."

Her eyes widened. "You do?"

He thought she was joking, but as he looked into her eyes he realized she wasn't, that for some reason, she thought he found her undesirable.

"Amy, if you knew how hard it was for me to hold back the other day, you would not be saying that."

"But I thought…"

"What?"

She looked down. "That you didn't want me, not like that. That maybe my belly turned you off—"

He kissed her. He didn't know why. Or maybe he did. Maybe it was the only way he could prove to her just how badly he wanted her. He kissed her and pressed himself up against her, showing her what she did to him, and she gasped. His tongue slipped inside her mouth and just like before, he couldn't seem to get enough of her, tipping his head sideways, suckling her and twining his tongue with her own, a part of him wondering how in God's name she could have thought he didn't want her.

Somehow, he would never recall how, he backed her though the tiny family room and into the bedroom. He'd tugged her shirt off before he'd closed the door, and even though he wore a button-down, he somehow managed to get that off, too. He'd been wearing a cowboy hat at some point. Maybe. He couldn't remember. All he wanted was Amy. Naked Amy. And his bed. With her beneath him.

She was helping him now, undoing her pants, sliding them down. They both kicked off cowboy boots at the same time. She undid her bra, he slid off his jeans, but before she could pull down the tiny pink panties she wore, he knelt down in front of her, nuzzling her warm center, a move that caused her to groan and clutch his head.

Didn't want her. Was she crazy?

She sank to the bed. He kept nuzzling her and kissing her and driving her closer and closer to the edge. He could tell by the way her body began to shake and the way her moans grew louder and louder, but this wouldn't be like the last time. Oh, no. She didn't think he wanted her, but he would show her just what she did to him.

He slid up her body, kissing her belly again, the muscle contracting beneath him, then her bare breast, circling her nipple with his tongue. She began to writhe beneath him, but then he realized it wasn't just because of his effect on her. No. She was shucking off her panties somehow, which he really wished she wouldn't do because he wanted to slow things down.

Or did he?

Because suddenly she was naked beneath him and all he wanted—oh, how he wanted—was to thrust into her, but he couldn't do that because she was pregnant and he might hurt the baby. Or something. He didn't know. All he knew was he wanted to feel the exquisite warmth of her wrapped around him, and suddenly he was afraid.

"Can we…? Is it okay?"

"Yes," she groaned, thrusting her hips toward him.

"But I don't have protection."

"You're not going to get me pregnant," she all but yelled.

"Yeah, but—"

"Just shut up and get on with it," she ordered.

And he wanted to laugh, or maybe cry, or maybe do both those things because she drove him absolutely nuts. But then she wrapped her legs around him, drawing him ever closer and he was lost, just lost.

"Flynn," she panted. "Please."

She was all that he'd fantasized about and more. In a moment he knew he would never forget, Flynn sank into her, moaning her name at the same time.

She went wild beneath him. He wanted to tell her to slow down, but her movements and the warmth of her and the feel of her hardened nipples against his chest—he could no more have slowed down than he could reverse a wave crashing onto shore. Their mouths found each other, Flynn's hands sliding beneath her, pressing her closer, his tongue diving deeper and deeper, their bodies straining toward one another, tighter and tighter, higher and higher.

She jerked her lips away. "Flynn."

That was it. That was all he needed to hear. The sound of her crying out his name. The feel of her body around his own. He gasped, thrust his head back, and he knew in that instant that his life would never be the same again. He knew that because when they were finished, as she lay spent in his arms, he pulled her tight, as tight as he'd ever held a woman, his eyes closed—her eyes closed, too—his heartbeat slowly returning to normal.

"I have a feeling we're going to be late to Thanksgiving dinner," he heard her say.

It made him smile. She always made him smile.

"I think you're probably right."

He kissed her again and quickly proved her words true.

They rushed to get to dinner, although they ended up driving to save time, and contrary to Amy's fears, nobody seemed to notice their late arrival, which was good because she had to work to keep the sappy grin off her face.

"Just put those in the kitchen," called out Crystal, obviously spotting them from the family room, where she sat with easily half a dozen people. "We'll bake them for a few minutes when the turkey comes out."

It smelled heavenly in the house, and as odd as it might seem, Amy felt a little homesick all of a sudden. The apartment she'd shared with her mom was long gone, but it hadn't been all that bad. There'd been times when she'd felt loved and happy and content.

"I'm going to go find my brother," Flynn said, scanning the area around them. "Someone called about his horse. Think they might make him an offer."

She smiled. "Of course. Go."

He turned away and she watched him go, wondering at the odd pang of disappointment she'd felt before realizing it was because he hadn't kissed her goodbye or touched her or shown any sign that they were more than friends.

"You look lost."

Charlotte had come up alongside her and Amy was

glad for the distraction. It was nice to see a friendly face in the house full of strangers.

"I feel a little like a fish out of water."

Charlotte smiled. "They're a little overwhelming at first, aren't they?"

"At first?"

She laughed and smiled. "You'll get to know them, and then you'll wonder how you could have ever felt like a stranger."

They stood near the island that took up a large part of the kitchen. On the countertop were numerous appetizers and side dishes, so many Amy wouldn't have a clue where to start. It all looked so yummy.

Her eyes landed on Flynn. It was like his body was a giant pillar of steel and her eyes magnets that were naturally attracted to him. In his cowboy hat and jeans he looked much the same as the rest of his brothers and cousins, and yet different. His brothers were broad shouldered and tall. Flynn was skinnier and shorter than the rest of them, his height the same as his father. Still tall, but not like Maverick or even their father.

"Come on," said Charlotte. "Let's go outside. It's quieter there."

When she glanced back at Charlotte, it was just in time to catch a glimpse of something in her eyes, something that put Amy on alert. Did she know? Had she guessed? But she meekly followed her from the room, waving at Jayden, who sat by a man who must be her husband, Colby.

Charlotte was right. It was much quieter outside, the stark difference in sound like plunging into a swimming pool.

"You can't beat the view, can you?" Charlotte asked.

"No." Beneath them the vineyard stretched for what

seemed like miles. To their left, she could just make
out the roof of a house, probably Flynn's dad's place.
Beyond the valley, there were pastures and oak trees
and dirt roads that crisscrossed the landscape.

"Have a seat," she said.

There was a massive bench, one with tractor wheels
for the sides, the bottoms sawed off so they didn't roll
down the hill. For a moment Amy lost herself in imagining what that might look like, the two of them rolling down the hill on that bench, and it made her smile
as she sat down next to her new friend. That was what
Charlotte had become in recent weeks, a friend and a
mentor of sorts, and certainly her biggest cheerleader.
But that was the kind of person Charlotte was, Amy
supposed. She worked in Child Protective Services and
Amy knew she had to be brilliant at her job. She was
too warm and compassionate not to be. Maverick was
a lucky man, as was their daughter, Olivia.

"You slept with him, didn't you?"

Amy jerked. She turned to face Charlotte on the
seat next to her.

"Don't bother answering. I can see you did." And to
Amy's surprise, Charlotte started laughing.

"What's so funny?"

"I told Maverick this would happen." She shook her
head. "He didn't believe me. Said his brother would
never get involved with a woman carrying another
man's child, and I told him he was wrong. No man
would care about that sort of thing when they're as cute
as you, but he thought I was crazy, and now he owes
me twenty dollars."

Amy didn't know what to say. Actually, she did. "You
bet your husband that Flynn would sleep with me?"

Charlotte had the grace to look abashed. "Well, not

really sleep with you. Just that you'd end up together."
She frowned. "Hmm. That does sound kind of bad." Her
face cleared. "But whatever. I think it's great."

Amy shouldn't be surprised that Charlotte supported
her, but she couldn't keep a frown from creeping across
her face. No matter what she told herself, it'd really
bothered her that Flynn had slipped away without so
much as a peck on the cheek.

"What's wrong?" Charlotte asked.

She rested her hands on her belly, staring off into the
distance. "This isn't going to work out."

She felt a hand land on her arm. Charlotte's look of
concern was nearly her undoing. "What makes you say
that?"

She shrugged. "What happened just now, when we
came in." She bit her lower lip. "Did you see the way
he acted as if nothing had happened? But it's more than
that," she said.

Just staring at the vista below her served as a stern
reminder of what she was up against. Flynn came from
money. Maybe not his own, but he'd had the love and
support of his family for his entire life. She'd had to claw
her way to the top. But it wasn't that she didn't think
Flynn worked hard, because he clearly did. It was more
that their two worlds were so different. And then there
was the whole having-a-child thing. She'd have to be
stupid not to recognize what a terrible strain that would
put on a relationship, especially one that was just beginning. And then there was the craziness of her job. What
kind of man would put up with ten thousand Christmas
ornaments hanging from a family room curtain? Okay,
not really ten thousand, but close enough. Clearly, her
crazy life had driven Trent away, and others, too. Why
would Flynn be any different?

"I think you're selling yourself too short," Charlotte said, pulling her legs up so that she could wrap her arms around her knees. "Let me tell you a story."

Amy glanced over at Charlotte. She was staring out at the horizon and she realized Charlotte was really, really pretty in a way not many women could pull off. A natural beauty that didn't come from just the symmetry of her face, but from something that welled up inside.

"I grew up in foster homes," she admitted. "Some were good and some were very, very bad." She shook herself a bit, then turned to look Amy in the eyes. "It left scars. Not the physical kind, but emotional ones, and they ran deep. I thought that I would never marry or get involved with a man or have kids. But then I met Maverick and here was this wonderful man who didn't care about my past. And his family. Whew. They were all so sweet and kind and so happy to welcome me into their ranks, but deep inside, I didn't feel worthy. But Maverick made me see that I did have value, and that I shouldn't let my past get in the way of my future."

It was Amy's turn to look away and to stare out at the horizon. "But you weren't pregnant."

Charlotte huffed. "No. I wasn't. But that won't matter, not if Flynn loves you."

And that was just it. They'd made love and Amy had fallen ever closer to the precipice of love, but Flynn? He'd kissed her and held her tenderly, but there'd been no heartfelt declarations, not that she'd expected any, especially not with her track record with men. She'd just sort of thought...

"Thank you for sharing that with me," she said to Charlotte. "I'll try to keep the faith."

"Do," her friend said emphatically. "Don't be like me and push him away."

But when they went back inside and she spotted Flynn standing by a massive table that'd been set up on one side of the house, he barely looked at her. Granted, he was talking to his dad, but their gazes met and there was no smile, and no waving her over. Nothing but a quick glance. She told herself she was being a ninny. That it didn't mean anything. He was just busy and she was feeling clingy, probably because she was in a house full of people she barely knew. A lot of people would feel the same way.

"All right, everyone," Flynn's aunt Crystal said an hour later. "Let's all sit down and eat."

The word *eat* instantly perked her up. It seemed like these days she couldn't get enough food. It didn't matter that there were times when she'd barf it up later, the little girl inside her insisted on being fed at all hours of the day.

"Wow," she said when she spotted the spread laid out on the table in front of her. "That's a feast fit for a king."

Someone laughed. Shane, she realized, another of Flynn's brothers, his wife standing next to him, their twins already seated in high chairs. They were only a year or so older than Maverick's daughter, Olivia; all of the Gillian kids were seated at the table, too. It was a little overwhelming to have so many people she didn't know staring at her. Her eyes sought out Flynn's, but he wasn't even looking at her. He was still talking to Maverick, and from what she could hear, discussing horses. Flynn's uncle picked up the platter that held pieces of turkey, and that seemed to be the cue for other people to start serving themselves before passing the dish to the next person. Before she knew it, she had a plate full of food, and although she felt so tense and out of place, her stomach grumbled. Some things never changed.

Someone tapped the side of their glass. Flynn's aunt. She sat next to Uncle Bob and she smiled in her direction.

"Okay, so before we say blessings and dive into our food, I just want to welcome our guest, Amy."

One of Flynn's cousins lifted a glass and Amy smiled and tried not to hide beneath the table. She glanced at Flynn again, but he was staring at his plate, and for the first time since she'd met him, she felt a keening sense of disappointment. It wasn't that she'd expected him to take her hand and introduce her around as his girlfriend. Their relationship—or whatever they wanted to call it—was too new and too tenuous for bringing her home to Dad, so to speak. But she did expect more. A smile maybe. Heck, at this point, she'd settle for a wink.

She was so lost in thought that all she did was nod her head for the blessing. And when it came time to eat, she dug in, but she would never be able to name anything she tasted. By the end of the meal, she was so uncomfortable that she was the first person to volunteer to clear dishes. And then she found herself washing them. After which she helped put everything away. When, at last, she had nothing left to do she turned to Crystal and mentioned leaving.

"But you can't go home," she said. "We haven't even had dessert."

Dessert? Her interest perked, but then she quashed it down. She had to stop eating 24/7. At this rate, they'd have to roll her into the delivery room.

"Actually, I'm thinking the walk would do me good. I ate way too much." She added a smile. "And it was delicious."

"Well, thank you, but I still think you shouldn't walk. It'll be dark soon."

"Yeah, but it doesn't take me long—"

"Flynn," called Crystal. "Amy wants to go home.

Be a dear and take her, would you? If you don't, she's threatening to walk."

She hadn't even noticed Flynn had entered the kitchen, and she felt her cheeks heat when she met his gaze. Clearly, he didn't want his family to know about them, and that was okay with her. But she hoped he didn't think she was trying to force him into spending time with her or something.

"Sure," he said. "I can do that."

"It's really no trouble for me to walk," she said.

He shook his head. "Crystal's right. It'll be dark soon. Plus, I brought you up here. I can take you home."

"Exactly," Crystal said. "Go, you two. I'll save some dessert for you, Flynn."

But when she stepped outside, the first thing she said was, "You don't have to do this."

"No, it's okay."

She waited for him to touch her. To maybe place his hand on the small of her back. Give her some indication that their time together hadn't been forgotten, but all he did was open the door of his truck and wait for her to climb inside.

He'd hurt her feelings.

But as he crossed in front of her, never once looking in her direction, she knew he'd been trying to protect them somehow. That he'd guarded their relationship because he didn't want to answer questions, and that, at the root of it all, he was probably trying to save her from feeling awkward.

"We need to talk," she said.

"Yes," he said. "We do."

Chapter 17

She didn't say anything while he backed his truck out of the driveway, pointing it down the hill. That was good, Flynn thought. Gave him time to form an apology because he could tell she was hurt.

"They don't have to know what's going on between us, you know," he said.

"I know," she answered right back. "But it's too late, anyway."

"What do you mean?"

She peered over at him and the look in her eyes, it reminded him of when they'd first met, only this time he was the one who'd disappointed her.

"Charlotte," she said. "She guessed."

Son of—

"But don't worry. She won't say anything."

"Yeah, but—"

If Charlotte had guessed, that meant Aunt Crystal

might, too, and if she figured it out, it was only a matter of time before the whole family knew.

"If you'd wanted to keep it quiet about us, you should have warned me," she said. "I could have told Charlotte she was wrong." She looked out the window.

"I'm sorry," he said. "When I walked into my aunt's house and everyone turned to look at us, I just sort of freaked out. I wasn't ready to announce to the world that we were a thing."

She nodded, but she still wouldn't look at him. He reached across the seat, grabbed her hand. "I'm sorry. I should have explained my feelings in private."

She nodded again.

"No, really. I should have said something, pulled you to the side and explained, but I was afraid someone would see us together and start asking questions, and I just wasn't ready for that yet."

"I understand."

But did she? He wasn't certain he understood himself.

"Can I make it up to you? Bring you back some dessert in a little bit? Take you out to dinner one day this week?"

"What if someone in town sees us and tells your family?"

It was a valid point. "Then I'll just have to suck it up and tell them that you and I are dating."

"Suck it up?"

"I didn't mean that the way it sounded."

"And when I'm bigger? When it's obvious to all your friends that I'm pregnant? Will you want to take me out then?"

Her question struck a nerve, one that thrummed along his nerve endings and made him wonder if she sensed something he didn't. What would it be like to answer questions about her pregnancy? The invariable curiosity about how far along she was and if he hoped it would be a boy or a girl? And the awkward explanations that would follow.

"That's a long ways off."

"No, Flynn, it's not. In another month I'll be showing. Not a lot, but enough that people will guess what's going on. What, then?"

"I don't know," he answered honestly. "I haven't really thought about it."

They lapsed into silence and he wondered if he really was ready for this. Tonight had been a huge eye-opener for what he faced. And that was just his family.

"Maybe we ought to slow things down," she said. "Take a break."

He didn't want to slow down, though. He liked things just the way they were. Friends and now lovers.

"That's not necessary."

"Yes, I think it is." He heard her take a deep breath. "I think I'm falling in love with you, Flynn."

He hit the brakes. She thrust a hand out, stopping herself from sliding off her seat.

"Sorry," he said.

She just shook her head, her hand falling into her lap again. "I think I'm falling in love with you and I need to know, Flynn, if you're going to be there for me in the long run, or if this is just some kind of fling for you. A detour from your usual reality. Something to fill your time while you're waiting for something better to come along, because I have to tell you, that's not what this is for me."

He didn't know what to say.

Falling in love.

She couldn't mean that. They barely knew each other.

But as he turned and stared out his front windshield, he admitted that he knew her better than he'd known a lot of his girlfriends in the past. He knew that she liked hip-hop music and that she enjoyed bacon with her eggs and that when nobody was looking, she danced around the house. She enjoyed climbing trees and turning ordinary objects into works of art, and that, in her opinion, everything could be improved with a little bit of glue and *a lot* of glitter.

"I don't know what to say," he admitted out loud.

"Then don't say anything. Think about it."

But as he drove her home, his heart slamming against his rib cage, he wondered if he was up to it. But then he glanced at her, and the way she stared at him, with a look of hope and uncertainty and fear, he knew that it was worth it, or that it would be in time.

He stopped her with a touch. "I'm not going to hurt you, you know," he said.

"Not intentionally," she answered right back. She shook her head and her lips flattened as she lost herself in thought for a minute, and Flynn would have given anything to know what was going on in her head. "I know you would never do anything to me on purpose, Flynn. But I'm glad this happened now, early on in our relationship. Maybe you need to think about what you're in for." She waved at her belly. "And maybe I need to think about it, too. Both of us." She looked him in the eyes. "I don't want to get hurt again."

She slipped out of his truck.

"I'll call you," he said.

She didn't look like she believed him. "Okay."

She stepped back and he looked away, clutching the steering wheel as if holding on to it for dear life…and maybe he was.

* * *

Amy shut her front door and leaned up against it, closing her eyes. Still, as she listened to him drive away, a part of her hoped he'd change his mind.

Pick me, she silently chanted. *Pick me, pick me.*

But why would he do that? Trent hadn't. Neither had any of her other previous boyfriends. Why would Flynn be any different? Different from her own mother, who'd moved so far away? Not that she blamed Flynn. It was a lot to ask. She wasn't just asking him to be a boyfriend. She was asking him to be a daddy, too. To be there for her in a way most men wouldn't have to experience until they were married to the women of their dreams, and clearly she wasn't that to Flynn.

Not yet. Maybe not ever.

The next morning, when she still hadn't heard from him, she sat out on the porch, leaned her head against the post and tried not to cry. She told herself to be patient. She needed to give him time, but every second of every minute that turned into hours was agony for her, and in the back of her mind she still kept wondering if maybe her mom was right. Maybe no man would ever want her again.

So when, later, she heard the familiar clop of a horse's hooves, her heart rate shot up so fast it was like she'd been injected by a shot of adrenaline. She wobbled when she stood up. Only it wasn't Flynn. The man in the cowboy hat was Maverick.

"Flynn told me he rides this way," he said when he spotted her standing there like a lovelorn fool. "I just followed the tracks."

Love.

Yes, she admitted. She wasn't falling in love with Flynn. She was *in* love with him. No sense in denying it. Not anymore. And, damn, that had happened fast. Of course, she shouldn't be surprised. She had a habit of falling head over heels. And, yet, this time… This time it seemed very, very different.

"How's it going?" she asked, trying to act as if inside she wasn't shattering into a million little pieces because if Maverick was riding that meant he'd seen Flynn and if he'd seen Flynn, Maverick had probably told him where he was going, which meant he didn't want to ride over to see her.

"Good," Maverick called. "Trying to ride off some of that Thanksgiving dinner."

Or maybe she was overthinking things. Maybe Maverick had saddled up his horse at his place or something.

"Tried to get Flynn to ride over with me, but he's too busy."

The words were an arrow to the heart. He hadn't called this morning. She'd been hoping that he'd at least do that, but he hadn't, and it hurt, damn it.

"That's too bad," she said, still trying to act as if it was no big deal. Had Charlotte told him what had happened between them? Was he just playing along? Acting as if he didn't know?

Maverick dismounted, tying his horse up in the same spot as Flynn did. The tree with the low-hanging branch. And a new thought penetrated. Maybe Flynn had sent his brother over to her. Maybe Maverick was Flynn's emissary.

Flynn wanted me to tell you he'd like to be friends.

Flynn was wondering if you could forget the whole making-love thing.

Flynn doesn't ever want to see you again.

And the thing was, Maverick looked so much like Flynn that it hurt all the more watching him walk toward her. And what was it with the Gillian brothers that they always seemed to find her sitting on her porch, trying not to cry?

"Rough night?" he asked.

Did she look that bad? "Didn't sleep."

"I'm not surprised."

So, did he know? She wanted to ask. But at the same time, she didn't want to ask.

Maverick sat down next to her. "Charlotte said you seemed upset when you left last night, and that my aunt had to practically force Flynn to take you home."

He knew. Charlotte had made him pay his twenty dollars.

"Not exactly," she said, inhaling and hoping like hell her stupid hormones wouldn't get in the way of her resolve. But she couldn't help it. Having Maverick here made her want to bawl her eyes out and she had no idea why. Except…maybe she did. Maybe she was just really wishing Flynn had taken up Maverick's offer to ride over to see her. Maybe the fact that he didn't was all the proof she needed that it was over between her and Flynn.

Over before it really even began.

"He's scared," Maverick said.

She didn't need to ask who he was talking about. "Well, I am, too."

Damn it. She had to wipe at a renegade tear that made a run down her cheek.

"Yeah, but Flynn is a single man. One who's been living his life exactly according to plan for years. Then suddenly *you* come along and turn his whole life upside down."

"Me?" And despite her tears, she huffed out a laugh. "Gee, thanks."

"He's just afraid. I mean, he's the one who studies the pedigree of every single horse we bring onto the property, figuring out who will cross well on what stallion and who won't, and patiently waiting for the foals to drop in the spring, and then studying them and working with them and deciding which ones are good enough to go on to compete. And he's good at it. He's turned the horse breeding operation into a huge success. Some of the best cutting horses in the world reside right here at Gillian Ranch because of my brother. He's meticulous about everything he's ever done, except where you're concerned. With you he jumped in feetfirst without even thinking about it, and that's not like him."

Tissue. She needed tissue. Frankly, she should just get in the habit of stuffing wads of them in her pocket for moments like these.

"Give him time," he said. "Time to accept the fact that his well-ordered universe is about to be knocked back on its you-know-what."

She didn't have time, though. Every week her belly would get bigger and bigger and it would be an in-your-face reminder that she would one day give birth to another man's child. And if he came back to her, that meant he'd have a child, too. He'd have to put up with milk-jug boobs and a flabby belly and goodness knew what else that would happen to her body postpregnancy. A hot mess—just as Maverick said.

"Okay," she said. "I'll try not to go all *Fatal Attraction* on him."

Maverick stared at her in puzzlement.

"It's a movie." She shook her head. "Never mind. I'll give him some space."

Maverick slapped her on the knee. "Good. Because I like you, Amy. You have some crazy ideas about weddings, but you're exactly what Flynn needs. Someone who's just a little bit on the wacky side to counter his stick-in-the-mud attitude."

"Wacky?"

"In a good way," he said with a smile, standing. "I'll tell him I saw you. And that you had some guy over here. That ought to get his goat."

"Don't you dare."

"Oh, I will. I'll get Jayden to play along, too. And Crystal. The whole family. Just leave it to me. Operation Freak Out Flynn is underway."

He started walking backward toward his horse. The whole family? *Operation Freak Out Flynn?*

"Wait, I mean. Don't lie to him or anything."

"I'm not going to lie. Come over to the house next week for dinner."

"I can't. I have a wedding."

"Then the week after," he said, still walking backward. "Friday. We'll do dinner. I'll arrange it with Charlotte. In the meantime, don't you dare text Flynn. Don't call him, either. Don't do anything. Just let him sit and stew."

She wasn't so sure that was a good idea. Then again, maybe that was what he wanted. Maybe that was why he hadn't called her or sent her a text. Maybe he really did want to be left alone.

Maybe she would just have to get used to a life without Flynn.

Chapter 18

He'd behaved like a total putz.

Flynn rolled over in bed and immediately reached for his phone. He'd given it a day, a day during which it'd taken everything he had not to text her or call her. One day. That was all he lasted.

He scanned his bedroom, tugging on jeans while he looked for his phone, and tapped out a quick message.

I'm in.

He drew in a deep breath. At that moment, the precise second he pressed Send, he realized how much the whole thing had been weighing on him. How much he'd missed her…and what a prize ass he'd been.

He waited for a reply. When nothing happened, he finished dressing. Still nothing. He made himself some breakfast. Nothing.

I'm in for the whole shebang, he texted next.

She was probably doing something weddingish. Maybe in a meeting. No need to stress. So he went to work, checked the horses, made sure their automatic waterers were working, threw some of them extra food. Rode two, stepped into his office where he kept his phone when he rode the horses, and checked again. Still nothing.

It wasn't until later that night that he finally received a reply.

I'll call you later.

She was mad at him; he could tell. She had a right to be, but the thing was, she didn't strike him as the type to string him along or be vindictive. One of the things he admired about her was that she never held back. She always told the truth. Seemed to pride herself on speaking her mind.

"Later" turned out to be not the same day, or even the next one. He ended up hearing from Maverick that she was out of town. Some big wedding she'd been planning. That was when he remembered the ornaments and the December wedding and he felt a little bit better, but only a little.

He swung by her place. She wasn't home. Her car was missing, too, so he knew his brother must be right. Out of town. Working a wedding. She'd call him when she returned home.

Except…she didn't. He went by her place again, but she wasn't home and this time he heard from Jayden that she'd had a doctor's appointment and that his own sister had taken her to it. Funny how upset that made him. And when Amy did finally call, he missed it, but the message she left worried him all the more. She'd talk to him later this weekend, she said. That was it.

This weekend.

He didn't know what to think, called his brother to see if maybe he knew what was going on, and when he was told to stop in for dinner that same night because Amy would be there, he leaped at the chance. Maybe Amy had shared her feelings with Maverick and Charlotte. He sure hoped so because he'd never felt more at a loss in his whole life.

There were cars in the driveway, one of them causing his grip to tighten on the steering wheel. Amy. The porchlight illuminating her beat-up little car. There were more cars than just Amy's, though. And the sound of voices coming from inside the house made it sound as if they were having a party, not a little get-together. Laughter. A glass tinkling. Music.

"Flynn," his brother said, opening the door after he'd knocked.

He stepped inside. Not a party, he realized. Just a little get-together. And a man sitting across from Amy, someone he didn't recognize. He waited for Amy to turn and look at him, but she didn't move.

"This is Ryan," Maverick said, guiding him forward. "He works with Charlotte. And, of course, you know Amy."

Ryan unfolded himself from his chair. He was tall and he wore tan slacks and a casual white button-down. Flynn hated him on sight.

"Hi, Flynn. Nice to meet you." He smiled and Flynn wondered if Ryan heard the way his teeth cricked together when they shook hands. "I'm actually one of Charlotte's foster dads, so I don't really work with her."

A foster dad? Wasn't that unethical or something? To socialize with a CPS worker?

"Where's Olivia?" Flynn asked.

"Up with Aunt Crystal," Maverick answered. "She's watching Ryan's little girl, too. They're having a blast playing together."

He had a little girl. And he was single. Flynn noticed the fact that he didn't have a ring on his finger, and if ever Flynn had doubts about his feelings for Amy, they disappeared the moment he looked deep into the man's eyes. He didn't know him. For all he knew he could be the world's best dad, but the stab of jealousy he felt as he smiled into Flynn's eyes was undeniable.

"Would you like a beer?" Maverick asked as Ryan returned to his chair. Amy had yet to look at him.

"No, thanks."

"Hey, Flynn," Charlotte said, offering her cheek for him to kiss. "Glad you could make it."

"Take a seat," Maverick said.

"No, thanks. I'm actually only here to talk to Amy."

She finally looked into his eyes and for the first time since he'd met her, he couldn't tell what she was thinking. She just stared up at him, and he hated that he'd stolen the smile from her eyes.

"Can I talk to you outside?" he asked.

Her lashes lowered for a second, but she held his gaze. "Sure."

He headed toward the back porch and as he passed by his brother he saw his raised eyebrows, but there was also something else in the blue depths of his gaze, a mischievousness that he instantly recognized from their childhood. He'd set the whole thing up. The invitation. The dinner. The other man.

Bastard.

Or maybe not. Maybe he should thank him because something told him Amy might have gone on avoiding him for a while longer if he hadn't caught her here tonight. He wondered if Maverick had told her he was coming over. Probably not. Or maybe. His insides were so turned upside down that he had no idea what to think anymore.

"It's chilly out," she said.

He paused midstep. "Do you need me to go inside and get you a jacket?"

She shook her head and he took her to the back porch, pointing to the wooden chairs his brother Carson had built, their seats covered by cushions. He took one. She took the other, the two of them staring out at a backyard softly lit by moonlight. This time of year, the cilantro-like scent of hedge parsley filled the air. In the summer those plants would dry and the resulting burrs would get caught in Sadie's fur.

"You want to go or shall I?" she asked.

He kept his gaze focused on the wooded area off the back of his brother's house. They'd yet to landscape, but a swing had been added in recent weeks.

"I don't know what to say," he said, shaking his head. "Except I'm sorry. I'm not ashamed of you, if that's what you're thinking. Ashamed of us," he quickly amended. "I think I was just afraid. It suddenly hit me what dating you meant. A commitment, not just to you, but to your baby. I didn't know how I'd fit into it all. If we'd go back to being friends or what. But then you said you were falling in love with me and it scared me even more because I'm falling in love with you, too."

He expected a reaction from her, but she didn't move, and he thought at first it was out of shock, but then realized that wasn't it at all. His eyes had adjusted to the darkness, and the ambient glow emanating from inside the house provided just enough light for him to read the look on her face.

Sadness.

She shook her head as if answering his silent question of what the heck was going on, then turned and stared out at the backyard. He spotted something else, too. A tear that left a silver streak on her cheek, and his heartbeat took off running again.

"Two weeks ago, hearing you say those words… Whew." She took a deep breath. "They would have rocked my world."

"But now?"

"Now they rob me of breath for a different reason." She finally met his gaze. He could see pain in the depths of her eyes, and sorrow, and a grim determination that he'd never seen before.

"I can't do this, Flynn." She let him absorb the words for a moment before saying, "I can't keep running into the arms of men."

"What do you mean?"

"I haven't exactly been the patron saint of abstinence," she said.

He still didn't understand. His look must have said as much.

"Trent wasn't the first guy to dump me."

"So? I've been dumped before, too."

"I doubt that," she said. "You're too good-looking. Too kind. Too perfect in every way to be a man someone would walk away from. Heck. You have women who haven't seen you in years still lusting after you. I had to ask for a new ob-gyn because of you."

He wanted to deny it, but as he thought back on his past relationships, he realized she was right. He was usually the one who did the leaving. Funny. He'd never thought about that before.

"Then why are you dumping me?"

She shook her head. "You don't understand."

No, he didn't. "Help me."

She took a deep breath. "I have to stop doing this. I have to stop jumping into things. I can't keep doing what I'm doing, not when I have a baby girl to think of now."

"But you said you were falling in love with me."

"I'm not falling, Flynn, I am *in* love with you. I know it. You're the most amazingly perfect man I've ever met in my life, but I can't afford to make a mistake this time. I have more than myself to think of this time around. What if I'm wrong? What if my feelings are the by-product of hormones or something? I can't… I won't—"

He got up from his chair, knelt in front of her, clasped her hands and looked into her eyes. "And what if this is it?" he countered. "What if this is the real deal?"

She stared down at him, another tear in her eye. "Then I'm making the biggest mistake of my life, but I'll have made it for the right reasons."

He stood up, turned and faced the backyard again, more frustrated than he could ever remember feeling in his life. What was going on? Why was she pushing him away? Was it a game? Was this some kind of revenge?

But when he turned and looked at her again, as he stared down into her tearstained face, he realized she was absolutely and utterly serious. She was in love with him, but for some crazy, asinine reason, she felt it was better to call things off before they'd ever had a chance to really begin.

"Don't do this," he begged.

"I have to, Flynn. Don't you see? I have to think of

the baby. What's better for her? A mom who's so co-dependent on men she's never spent more than a couple weeks without one in her bed? Or a mom who's learned to stand on her own two feet? I need to learn who that woman is, Flynn. I need to see the person motherhood will make me become because the woman I am now may be completely different after the baby comes."

Her words left him speechless and heartbroken and a whole host of other emotions he couldn't put a name to. "Don't do this," he begged.

"I have to," she said. "I have to start being enough… enough for me and the baby."

Chapter 19

She didn't leave the party. She refused to run away. Instead she sat and watched as he walked inside, nodding to his brother and telling him he'd talk to them later, before exiting the house. And Ryan, poor Ryan, stared at them all as if trying to understand the punchline of a joke. Maverick and Charlotte exchanged glances before looking at her with confusion and surprise in their eyes.

She had no idea how she made it through the rest of the night. Somehow she held herself together, even though she crumbled inside because every single part of her, every little atom, wanted to run after him, to tell him that she was wrong. That she needed him. But that was the problem. She'd made so many mistakes in her life. So many poor choices. This time, for her baby's sake, she couldn't afford to be wrong.

So she let him go. And later that night, as she drove home, she pulled into her place and bawled her eyes out, and that made zero sense because she was the one to tell him goodbye. So why was she crying? And why did it feel as if she couldn't catch her breath?

"So that's it?" Jayden asked when they met for her baby shower two weeks later. "You're really done?"

No one else had arrived yet, which was good, because she'd already talked things over with Charlotte at least half a dozen times and she didn't want to go over everything yet again. Charlotte claimed Flynn was completely brokenhearted, but he hadn't exactly broken down her door to see her again, not that she blamed him. She'd been the one to give him the cold shoulder first, and then the one to call things off, so what did she expect?

But a part of her—a tiny little corner of her heart— wondered why, if he loved her, truly loved her, he wouldn't at least stop by or text her or leave her a voice mail message.

"We haven't spoken since that night."

The whole family knew about her and Flynn now. Even Aunt Crystal had mentioned it when they'd met to discuss the carriage she'd bought just for Maverick and Charlotte's wedding because, just as Charlotte had thought, the rental agencies were happy to rent them a carriage…as long as the Gillians used the rental agency's horses, which Crystal didn't want to do. So Crystal had purchased her own. To hell with them, she'd said. Amy had also learned to call it a coach and not a carriage because the two were completely different.

"Maverick says he's been moping around," Jayden said, tying off a balloon she'd just filled with helium. Pink for the little girl Amy carried.

Amy had been moping around, too, even though it was all her doing. She missed Flynn more than she

would have thought possible, had to stop herself from picking up the phone and calling him at least a dozen times a day. She'd gotten used to him always being around, but more than that, she missed her best friend.

"It's for the best," she told Jayden.

Jayden didn't look convinced. Funny, she wasn't all that convinced herself.

"Oh, dang. I forgot to warm up that artichoke dip." Jayden pushed herself up out of her chair. In recent weeks she'd sprouted a bona fide pregnancy belly, one that stuck out in front of her and reminded Amy that she'd look the same way in the not too distant future.

"Can you keep filling up balloons?" Jayden asked.

"Of course."

It'd been hard to take a back seat to the party planning, but she had to admit, it'd also been nice. Jayden's new house less than a mile down the road from her old job was absolutely stunning with its view of the Via Del Caballo valley and the mountains in the distance. The place was huge, probably too big for the meager number of friends Amy had.

Or so she thought.

Because as it turned out, nearly every bride she'd ever worked with ended up coming to her party. And not just the brides, but in some cases the bride's mother or sister or best friend. People she hadn't seen in forever showed up in support of her and the baby girl she carried, and it warmed Amy's heart. When she heard the doorbell ring yet again, she had no idea who it would be, but she truly didn't expect who she spotted at the door.

Her mother.

It took a moment for her to recognize the bleached-blond hair and the sun-bronzed face, which just went

to show how long it'd been. What was it? Two? Three years?

"You came," she said to the woman, who'd spoken to her exactly three times since she'd called her to tell her she was pregnant.

"Of course," said her mom. "I jumped at the chance to ride on a private jet."

Private jet?

"Colby insisted," Jayden said from behind her. "The family does a lot of business in Florida and so it's easy-peasy to pick someone up."

Amy swung back around to face her new friend. Easy-peasy? Just how much money did Jayden and Colby have?

"You should have seen it, honey," her mom said, coming into the foyer and looking around. "They sent a car to pick me up and bring me to this private terminal and everything. And there were two stewardesses on board and they brought me anything I wanted. You sure know how to pick friends. I was impressed."

Amy winced. Pick friends? The inference being, of course, that she was friends with Jayden because of her money.

"Mom, this is Jayden. She's part of the team of ladies who've been planning the shower."

"I know that already, silly. She introduced herself on the phone."

Because you couldn't be bothered to help out apparently.

She shook her head at the spitefulness of the thought. She refused to think like that even if it was true. Apparently, Charlotte had tried to talk to her mom about what she needed and the things Amy liked and she'd brushed them off. Amy hadn't been surprised, but Charlotte had

sounded a little disappointed. Par for the course for her mom. But she refused to dwell on it. It wasn't good for the baby to have negative energy around her.

"What a beautiful house you have, Jayden," her mom said, eyeing the massive family room to their left. One that, if you followed it around to the right, led to an equally massive kitchen. With three levels, an open floor plan and its mountaintop perch, the home was like a sparkling jewel set atop a crown. It was hard not to be jealous. Jayden couldn't be much older than Amy and she'd clearly found herself a prince of a man.

Oh, dear goodness. Two minutes in her mom's company and she was already sounding like her. See, that was why she'd had to keep away. Why she'd stayed behind when her mom had moved to Florida.

She closed her eyes, shook her head. No more.

"You're pregnant, too," observed her mom, pointing at Jayden's belly.

"I am," Jayden said brightly.

Her mom turned toward her. "Maybe you'll get lucky and look as good as Jayden does when you're that far along."

What to say to that?

Nothing.

That was the thing with her mother. She always made Amy feel so inadequate that she took a microscope to everything she said, twisting the words around and examining them to discover if there was an insult buried in there. She was pretty sure there was this time around, but *why did it matter*?

"Come on in," Jayden said. "I'll introduce you around."

"Looks like a lot of people came," said her mom. "I didn't know you had so many friends."

And off they went. Amy hung back, realizing her

mom had yet to hug her or kiss her or say a word about her own pregnancy, other than that one comparison to Jayden. It hurt.

Damn her.

Amy had known her mom had been invited, but she'd been certain she wouldn't show up. Obviously, she wouldn't have come if it hadn't been for her free ride on a jet. She could hardly blame her mom for wanting to do that, though.

Jayden introduced her mom to the others. Charlotte took Amy aside and forced a Mom-to-Be sash over her head. Amy drew the line at wearing a crown. The food was scrumptious and, for the most part, Amy was able to forget about her mom, although every once in a while she'd hear her say something that would make Amy wince. When she heard her mom discussing her high school pictures, and how she'd had to insist Amy take them again because they were so bad, she had to leave the room, hiding in the kitchen, although tempted to slip out the back.

"Your mom is…interesting," Ava said, having followed her. She held a pile of dishes. No paper plates for Jayden. Oh, no. She'd actually bought china that'd been hand painted with pink bows. The house had pink roses all over the place, too, their smell filling the air. It was all so beautiful Amy wanted to cry.

And then her mom had to come and spoil it all.

"She's totally toxic," Amy grumbled, then clapped a hand over her mouth, peeking over her shoulder to see if her mom had heard. But she was in the family room with the rest of the guests, thank goodness. "I can't believe I just said that. Sorry. I promised myself I'd project nothing but positive energy today."

"Yeah, but it all makes sense now," Ava said.

"What does?"

Ava looked into her eyes, her mouth opening as if about to say something, but then she changed her mind. "Nothing."

Amy stepped in front of her. "Oh, no. You can't say something like that and just walk away." She tipped her head. "What makes sense?"

Another measured stare, Ava leaning against the kitchen counter. "Your choice of career. Your complete dedication to your job. Your utter determination to ensure your brides have their happily-ever-afters. You lavish everyone with attention, Amy, making people feel special. It's why you have so many of your clients here today. When you're done planning their wedding, they end up feeling like a friend. And they *are* your friends. Look at Charlotte and the rest of us. You're one of the most generous and giving human beings I know, which is why it's so surprising you broke Flynn's heart."

Amy took a step back.

"I'm sorry. That wasn't what I meant to say." And Ava looked genuinely contrite. "Not really. I just meant you're always trying to prove yourself to everyone around you, and now I know why. And I think I know why you broke up with Flynn, too."

"Because of my mom."

Ava glanced around and motioned for her to follow. She led her to a sliding glass door, one that led to a deck overlooking the back of the house, which, because of the home's mountaintop perch, also had a view of the valley down below—just like the front. It might be winter, but the sun was shining and the grass was gleaming and it was hard to believe Christmas was right around the corner.

"Look," Ava said. "When I first met you, I have to

be honest, I was worried you were some kind of gold-digging jerk, someone looking for a baby daddy and nothing more."

Amy winced. "Oh, ouch."

"It's true. Aunt Crystal confessed to me she thought the same thing, too. But then I met you and I saw how hard you were working to make Charlotte's wedding day special, and I thought for someone looking for a meal ticket, you were working way too hard. And as I got to know you, I realized you weren't who I thought you were at all. You're sweet and generous and nice, and then later, I figured something had to be wrong if you would break Flynn's heart like you did. We've all talked about it. Jayden, Charlotte, Aunt Crystal and my-self. We're not mad at you or anything—don't look at me like that, we're not. We're just so baffled."

"I didn't mean to break his heart." Amy placed a hand on her chest. "I really didn't."

"I know. It was one of those things. But the poor man is hurting. Maverick says Flynn refuses to talk about it. He's devastated by your breakup and I guess that's pretty unusual for Flynn because normally he shrugs things off, especially where women are concerned. But you? With you it was different. He's been shutting down when your name is mentioned."

Amy didn't know what to say. She'd been so focused on her own misery she hadn't wanted to think about Flynn. But if he felt even a tenth of what she felt, she could only imagine how hard it was for him.

"And now it all makes sense." Ava tapped her head. "She's done a real number on you up here."

Amy sank into a chair, staring out at the vista be-yond. She wouldn't deny it. She'd held her mom up as an example of everything she didn't want to be enough times to know her upbringing had a lot to do with why she was the way she was. She hadn't wanted to be her mother. Hadn't wanted to subject her child to one failed relationship after another. That was what it'd been like for Amy growing up. A parade of men, some of them nice, some of them terrible, all of them leaving. Her mom had always blamed their leaving on her, she admitted, and it was funny because she'd never really thought about it before. Never really admitted to herself that by trying to avoid the same pitfalls, she'd actually ended up doing the same thing—she'd dated a string of men, none of them Mr. Right. But as she looked back through the history of her mom's romantic past, she realized it really was true. Her mom had always pointed the finger at her. The difference was when it came to Amy's own checkered past, she'd always blamed herself, not someone else. Except for Trent. But then she took a deep breath. Maybe Trent, too.

They just don't want kids.

They didn't like the fact that I always had you to drag along.

It scared them how much money raising a kid requires.

Jeez-oh-peets. No wonder she was so messed up.

She heard Ava sit down, too. A hand reached out and clasped her own.

"Amy, you aren't a mistake. You're a good person. And you're nothing, and I do mean *nothing*, like your mom."

A mistake? Was that how she thought of herself? Was that why she was so committed to having this baby? Because she wanted to prove her worth somehow? Was that why she'd broken up with Flynn? Because deep down inside—way, way down—she didn't feel worthy of him somehow? Was that why she'd always failed at relationships?

The hand squeezed her own. "Think about what I said."

She wasn't like her mom. But dear God…she worried she'd end up just like her. That her baby would somehow turn her into her. And she didn't want Flynn to see that.

"I'm an idiot," she muttered to herself.

"Yes, you are. But an adorable one. And I get it now." Ava shook her head, smiled. "Your mom. Whew. Some of the things that come out of her mouth. No wonder you have an inferiority complex."

Inferiority complex?

Yes, answered a little voice. She did feel unworthy. Of Flynn's whole family. That she would never fit in, not really, and deep inside she worried that they would always wonder if she'd gotten involved with him because she was pregnant.

"I really *am* an idiot," she muttered again.

"Yes, but the question is, what do you plan to do about it?"

Chapter 20

"All right, kid," Flynn said. "You ready for this?"

Olivia stared up at him for a second, clearly analyzing his words. Her brown hair, once so limp and flyaway, had been pulled back, a pink bow high upon her head, her ponytail bobbing as she moved her head up and down.

"Okay, then," Flynn said. "Let's do this."

He pushed open the door to The Toy Box, a boutique store with every kind of kid's toy imaginable, and a hub of activity this close to Christmas. Not that Olivia noticed. She gasped and looked around, her eyes so wide Flynn almost laughed. But then she spotted a giant stuffed teddy bear that sat front and center, a big red bow around its neck.

"Do you like that?" he asked.

Olivia nodded again and Flynn found himself on the verge of laughter. Just what he needed, he thought, to buy her a big old teddy bear. But he'd been enjoying his time with his niece. They were supposedly doing some last-minute Christmas shopping for his other nieces and nephews, but Flynn planned on getting ideas for Olivia, too, and that teddy bear would be perfect. But then Olivia spotted a whole shelf full of stuffed animals and Flynn resigned himself to buying Olivia something that day. Maverick had warned him before they walked out of his front door that a toy store was probably not the best location in the world to take a child when one was babysitting, but Flynn hadn't cared. He'd needed the distraction.

Three weeks.

It'd been three long weeks since that fateful night with Amy. Three weeks during which he'd thought about every last detail of their relationship. What had he done wrong? Why didn't she trust that things would work out between them? How had he fallen in love in such a short amount of time?

"Want," he heard Olivia say, and when he looked down, it was in time to see her point at something. He followed her gaze.

And looked straight into Amy's eyes.

Olivia tugged at his hand, clearly anxious to say hello to her friend. He tried to hang back, but the little girl wouldn't let him.

"Olivia," Amy said, smiling down at his niece. She squatted and gave the child a hug. "What are you doing here, honey?"

He hated that she wouldn't look at him. Then again, could he blame her? He didn't exactly want to see her, either. But he could be the bigger person. And so he pasted a smile on his face.

"I think she's about to empty my wallet," he admitted.

He watched as Amy took a deep breath, stood again, and when she met his gaze it made him dizzy—physically, crazily dizzy—and he realized that he could read her eyes again, could see the sadness and the regret and something else that he couldn't immediately identify but that made his heart skip a beat for some reason.

"You're a better man than I am, Gunga Din," she quoted, smiling down at Olivia again.

She'd popped. Her belly, once barely noticeable, had definitely graduated from baby bulge to baby bump status. He wondered if she'd thought of a name. Wondered what kinds of things she'd gotten at her baby shower the other day. Wondered if she'd made amends with Trent. So many things—none of it his business.

"What are you here for?" he asked.

Her expression turned sheepish. "Would you believe wedding decorations?"

It was just like before. Her silly grin. The twinkle in her eyes. Damn, he'd missed her.

"Where you're concerned, I would believe anything."

"It's this whole *Toy Story* wedding theme. The bride and groom both work for an animation studio. Long story."

She smiled again, and he wished things were different. That at the very least they could still be friends.

"You want to go shopping with us?" he heard himself ask.

He had no idea where the words had come from, but he wished them back the moment he said them. Her eyes dimmed. She glanced down at Olivia.

"Nah. I don't want to intrude."

She squatted down again. "Goodbye, Miss Olivia." She kissed his niece on the cheek. "I'll see you after Christmas."

"Christmas!" Olivia echoed. Then pointed. "Toy."

"Yes. Christmas. I hope Santa brings you lots of toys."

What was the look in her eyes? Sadness? But this whole thing. The breakup. The silence. It was her idea.

"Goodbye, Flynn."

She turned and headed to the opposite corner of the store. Olivia tugged on his hand, wanting to go after her, but he scooped her up into his arms.

"You know what, kiddo? How about if we go get some ice cream before we shop?"

Olivia drew back, looking at him as if he'd announced he wanted to feed her spinach.

"We'll come back, okay?"

"No," Olivia said.

In for a penny, in for a pound.

"Come on. Let's go."

"No," Olivia shouted, louder.

"We'll be right back."

"No," she screamed.

He left before the decibel level climbed any higher, and he wondered if Amy watched him go. If she was watching him, she had to know he'd left because of her. And that was the moment Flynn realized his feelings for her hadn't changed a bit. They crippled him to the point that he'd drag Olivia out of a toy store, crying and upset, just so he wouldn't have to face her.

"It's okay, pumpkin, I'll bring you back."

"Want," Olivia said again, tears streaming, hands reaching out toward the store.

He knew exactly how Olivia felt.

She hid behind a shelf full of Barbies, watching as he dashed out of the store. Amy closed her eyes and rested her head against a pink-and-white box. Poor Olivia. She could hear her crying outside. And all because of her. She was half-tempted to go chasing after them, to tell him that she would be the one to leave, but when she stepped toward the store's front window and peered over the top of an electric train, he was already gone.

She would never remember picking up the toys on her list. She must have paid for them, too. At least she sure hoped so because if she didn't, she'd just shoplifted for the first time in her life. Somehow she made it home, too, staring at the blinking Christmas tree in her front room and feeling so bleak and lonely that if she'd been a different kind of person she might have drowned her sorrows, pregnancy or not. But she would never jeopardize the health of her child.

She didn't sleep very well that night or the next. The days marched toward Christmas and she wondered what Flynn was doing. She knew the Gillians were big on Christmas holidays. No doubt he was wrapping presents and spending time with his family.

A car pulled up.

And for a moment, a brief, breathtaking moment, her heart raced.

Flynn.

Only it wasn't Flynn. It was her mother.

Oh, damn.

She'd known she was probably still in town. The plan had been for her to go back home just before Christmas. She'd left her baby shower confessing her intention to turn her trip into a sightseeing tour, a Christmas present to herself, and Amy hadn't protested. Strangely, the fact that she hadn't wanted to spend time with Amy hadn't hurt. Well, not as much as she would have thought. Ava was right. It was time to stop feeling so sorry for herself.

"Mom," she said, forcing a smile on her face. "What are you doing here?"

Her mom's green eyes—so much like her own—widened. "What do you mean what am I doing here? I told you I would come by before I left."

Should she be hurt her mom didn't want to spend Christmas with her? Oddly, she wasn't.

"Come on in," she said, pasting a smile on her face.

Her mom took two steps into her place and paused. "Wow, Amy, this is really tiny."

She took a deep breath. "I know? Isn't it perfect?"

Her mom paused near the family room, which was also near the kitchen and her bedroom because, yes, her rental was really, really small. But it worked. And she was grateful for it.

But it never felt small when Flynn was around.

She had to stop thinking about him. Or maybe not. Maybe Ava was right. Maybe it was time to get her mother out of her head.

"Have a seat," she told her mom.

"Oh, no, I can't. I only came by to give you a hug and say goodbye and to give you this." She handed Amy a box she hadn't even noticed her carrying.

"What's that?"

"Open it up on Christmas Day." She glanced at the tiny tree in the corner of her family room. There weren't any presents under it.

"Well," Amy said before her mom could make a derogatory comment about that, "goodbye."

Her mom frowned. Amy stepped away, puzzled.

"Look, Amy, before I go, I wanted to apologize for some of the things I said at the baby shower."

"Oh?" Amy asked, playing innocent even though

inside she could have been knocked over with a feather. "What things?"

"Oh, you know. Inferring you'd gained weight. That you would have to work hard to be a good mother. That kind of thing."

She really did feel like she could fall over in shock.

"Your friends made me realize some of my words were a little insulting."

"My friends?"

Her mom nodded. "They took me aside afterward. Jayden, Charlotte, Ava. Even that famous race-car driver who showed up late. What's her name? Kait? She was in on it, too, although you didn't have to sic them on me like that."

"I didn't sic them on you."

"Sure, honey. You could have come to me and talked things out with me. You didn't have to make them be the bad guys."

Amy crossed her arms in front of her, although, perversely, she felt something rise inside her that she couldn't immediately put a name to.

"Mom, I didn't ask them to talk to you. If they pulled you aside, it was entirely their doing."

Her mom's bleached brows lifted in shock. "You must have said something to them."

Elation. That was what it was. And, and…she mulled over the emotions coursing through her. Gratitude. And love. She felt love toward her new posse of friends. They had taken the time out of their busy lives to defend her. To try to help her. To hold a looking glass up to her mom in the hopes that she would see herself in a different light.

God love them.

"I didn't say a word to them, Mom. Believe me. I'm used to your little barbs. They don't affect me anymore."

That was an out-and-out lie. They did hurt. They would always hurt. But maybe not so much anymore. Maybe she had finally begun to believe that there was no truth to most of them. That, for some reason, her mom had to say terrible things in order to make herself feel better.

"What do you mean?" her mom asked. "I don't always make digs like that. I might have said a few things at the party that didn't come out right, but I was tired from the trip. That's all."

Amy took a step back, finding the arm of her couch and perching on it. For the first time in her life she felt free, and it was the oddest sensation, this lightening of her spirits. She didn't care if her mom might be offended by what she was about to say. It really didn't matter to her anymore because she had people in her life who loved her just the way she was.

Including Flynn.

"Mom, don't take this the wrong way, but you're always super critical. I grew up always dodging your next little bomb."

Her mom opened her mouth. Amy held up a hand.

"It's true. Whether you see it or not, it's true. But I've realized in recent weeks that God made you the way you are for reasons only He can understand. And then God made me, and I'm perfect just the way I am, faults and all, because I know I have them."

You broke Flynn's heart out of fear.

Fear that she wasn't good enough. Fear of what her mom might think. Fear that he would break her heart. Just like Ava had inferred.

"I'm in love with Flynn Gillian," she admitted.

"Who?"

And Amy almost laughed. How perfectly ironic. Her first heartfelt vow of love and her mom didn't even know who he was.

"Jayden's brother," she said. "It's a long story, but I wanted you know. I'm in love with a man who's not my baby's father." She patted her belly. "And I broke his heart because I was stupid and afraid, but I'm not anymore. I'm at peace."

Her mom clearly didn't know what to say.

"Is he rich?"

And Amy laughed. She couldn't help herself. Some things would never change.

"Who cares if he's rich? Although, to be honest, I don't have a clue how much money he has. It doesn't matter. Don't you see? All that matters is that he loves me and I love him."

Free. She was soaring now.

"I have no idea if he'll ever forgive me, but I'm going to see if he will. But whatever happens, whether I end up with Flynn or not, if I deliver this baby with my friends by my side, or Flynn—if I'm alone or with my new family—you will be happy for me, Mom. And you will be kind. And you will support and love my baby and say kind things because if I catch you saying something negative around me ever again, I will send you home packing. Is that understood?"

"Amy. What are you talking about?"

"I'm talking about watching what comes out of your mouth, Mom. Thinking before you speak. Okay?"

"I'm not sure where this is coming from. You're the one who's too sensitive—"

"Hup-hup," Amy interrupted, wagging a finger at her. "That's what I'm talking about. That right there.

No more, Mom. I'm not sensitive. I'm your daughter and I have feelings, feelings that you will respect from here on out. Capisce?"

"Well, I suppose—"

"Yes or no, Mom?"

"Yes, I guess. I swear, sometimes you make no sense—"

"MOM."

Her mom jumped a little. But for the first time in her life, Amy saw guilt on her mom's face. Guilt and a dawning comprehension.

"Now. Go on back home. I'll call you next week. And you will be nice to me on the phone, okay?"

Her mom nodded. Amy almost laughed. Her mom must have realized it was better to keep her mouth shut at this point. Maybe she wasn't such a lost cause after all.

"I love you, Mom."

That, at least, garnered a reaction. "I love you, too, Amy. I hope you know that."

A week ago she might have wondered. But now, with her mom standing in front of her, Amy spotted the contrition on her face and realized that in her own way, her mom really did love her. She *was* worthy.

"Merry Christmas, Mom."

"Merry Christmas, honey."

They hugged again. Amy was surprised she wasn't crying.

"Go on, get out of here," she told her mom, turning her toward the door. "Thanks for the present."

"I'll be back before the baby's born," her mom said.

"God help us."

Her mom stopped. "Now who's being mean?"

Amy laughed, "Touché, Mom. Touché."

She walked her mom out, but after she'd waved her down the driveway, after she sat there for a moment mulling the whole thing over, she pulled out her phone. She pulled up Flynn's number by rote, selecting the text icon because she was too damn chicken to do anything else.

Sorry.

And then, after staring at the phone for a second, she typed, I love you.

Chapter 21

Flynn stared at the text for a full minute.

"What is it?" Maverick asked, shutting the stall door, the horse he'd just turned loose turning to face them both.

"Nothing," he said, tucking the phone back into his pocket.

I love you.

"You look like you've seen a ghost."

Maybe he had, he thought. In a way he had.

"Just Aunt Crystal wondering if we're coming up for Christmas Eve dinner tomorrow night," he lied. "I don't know why she'd ask that. We go every year."

Maverick's eyes narrowed. Flynn ducked his head.

"Yeah. That's strange. Especially since I was just up there and she didn't ask me a thing."

Okay, busted. But he didn't want Maverick asking questions. Not now. Not when he didn't know what to say or what to do or what it meant.

I love you.

What was she trying to tell him? He'd been half hoping she'd call him after they'd seen each other in the toy store. She hadn't and his spirts had sunk more and more each day, until…

What did it mean?

"Speaking of Christmas, I have no idea why you bought Olivia that huge teddy bear. She won't leave it alone."

He ducked his head again. "She wanted it."

After he'd dragged his niece out of the toy store he'd felt so bad that he found himself going back and spoiling her rotten. She hadn't seemed to mind, and he'd gotten his Christmas shopping done.

"Well, next time clear it with me, would you? The darn thing's too big for her bed. She insists on sleeping on it every night."

I love you.

Flynn followed his brother out to the parking lot, although his brother always walked from his home to the stables. For a brief second he considered showing Maverick the text, asking him what he thought it meant, but he chickened out at the last minute.

"I'll see you tomorrow, then, right?"

Flynn nodded, glancing up at the sky. Looked like rain. And it was cold. It rarely snowed in Via Del Caballo. The last time was twenty years ago, or so he'd heard on a newscast this morning, but it sure felt like it might.

"Maybe we'll get a white Christmas," he told his brother.

"That would make our nieces and nephews happy, that's for sure. You remember when we were kids and it did that? Man, it was fun sliding down that hill."

"I do remember."

One of the best days of his life.

I love you.

"I'll see you tomorrow, then," Maverick said.

Flynn waved, but he wasn't really paying attention. He turned back to the barn. He had a few last-minute things to do before he closed the stables for the Christmas holidays. Stalls to bed. Instructions to write. Calls to make.

When he got home that night he was exhausted, but he pulled out his phone and stared at it once more. Did she want to see him? Was that why she'd sent the message? Should he call her?

In the end, he took a deep breath, typing the words just before he went to bed.

I love you, too.

There. He'd done it. He'd confessed what was in his heart. The next move was hers, although he'd be lying if he didn't admit to staying awake half the night, listening for her, wondering if she'd walk to his place like she had before. She didn't and eventually he drifted off to sleep until the wee hours of the morning when the sound of a knock woke him up.

He sat there in bed, eyes open, heart pounding, telling himself not to get his hopes up. But he was kidding himself. He practically ran to the front door.

She stood there, bundled up in a thick jacket, and even though it was barely light out, he could spot how red her nose was from the cold.

"I fell asleep," she admitted.

He wore a shirt and cotton briefs and it was damn cold standing in his doorway. He barely noticed.

"I did, too."

"Yeah, but I didn't see your message until this morning."

"Oh."

They stood there, Flynn's heart beating so fast that it could have been sixteen below and he wouldn't have noticed. Nothing mattered but that she stood there in front of them, looking him in the eye and she seemed… different. Something had changed about her.

"Can I come in?" she asked, shivering.

He jerked back the door. "Yes. Of course. I'm sorry. I'm still half-asleep."

No, he wasn't. He'd jerked awake the moment he'd heard her knocking on the door.

She was here. In his home.

"My mom came by," she said, turning to face him, still bundled up in her jacket, hands tucked into pockets.

"Oh?" he asked.

"She gave me this." She pulled something out of her pocket. He couldn't make out what it was until she handed it to him.

An ornament.

It was flat and silver and he had to flip it over to see what it actually was. A picture frame, the words *Baby's First Christmas* on the front.

"That's me right there," she said, pointing. "I was supposed to wait until Christmas to open it, but I couldn't wait."

He stared at it in puzzlement. This gift, an old ornament, meant something to her. He didn't know why, but he sensed its importance.

"My mom brought it all the way from Florida." Her eyes had grown red and he knew her well enough that he knew she was on the verge of tears. "She kept it all these years."

"That's neat," he said because he didn't know what else to say. He knew what he wanted to do. He wanted to pull her into his arms. But she had come here to show him that, and he waited patiently to explain why.

"I was an ugly baby," she admitted.

He glanced down at the picture for a moment. "You were adorable."

She huffed with laughter. "Only someone in love with me could say that."

His breath caught for a moment. "I *am* in love with you."

"I know," she said, her voice having gone thick with tears. "When I saw you standing in that damn toy store, holding Olivia's hand, my heart leaped, Flynn. It just leaped into my throat and I couldn't move because the emotions I felt were so powerful they literally took my breath away. I saw you with Olivia and then I saw you in the future, holding my daughter's hand, and I wanted to cry because I wanted that so badly for Abigail."

He gasped.

Abigail.

"Is that going to be her name?" he asked through a throat gone thick with tears.

"Jayden told me that was your mother's name and it somehow seemed fitting. Abigail. Abby for short."

His mom's name. His own eyes filled with tears.

"My mom gave this ornament to me, something she'd held on to for years, and then I read the inscription on the back and I just wanted to cry."

He flipped the ornament over again. "Merry Christmas from the Jensens," he pretended to read.

"That's not what it says," she said, swiping the thing away from him and then laughing and crying and shaking her head.

"I know," he said, suddenly serious again. "I read it when you first handed it to me."

"When I think about my life and what I've done right, I'm thankful every day God gave me you," she recited.

"I'm thankful, too," he said.

"She had that inscribed before I talked to her." She met his gaze, her lashes holding on to her tears. "She came by yesterday and I told her she needed to be nicer to me and she tried—you could tell she was really trying there at the end to watch what she said to me. And the whole time she had this for me, and when I opened it and read it I cried, but that was after I sent you that text, not that it matters. The point is that my mom loves me. She really does. And I know that sounds crazy because every daughter knows their mom loves them, only I don't know that I really did—"

"Amy," he said, suddenly on the verge of laughter again. "You're rambling."

"Am I?"

He took a step closer to her. "You are. You always do when you're emotionally distraught."

"I'm not emotionally distraught, though. For the first time in my life, I realize that I'm enough. Big belly and all."

"It's not big."

"No, but it will be, and you're only saying that because you love me and you don't care what I look like."

He closed the distance between them. "No, I don't," he said, bending down and kissing her. "But you're right. You're enough for me. You and Abigail are all I want."

"Flynn," she said softly, looking into his eyes. "I've been such an idiot."

"So have I. I should have fought for you harder, should have fought for the woman I love."

"I love you, too, Flynn. I think I fell in love with you when you carried me into the house that first time I got sick. You're my knight in shining armor and I don't want to go another day without you in my life."

He pulled her toward him, holding her, his head resting on top of hers as he uttered, "Then don't." His gaze caught on his Christmas tree. "Stay with me for always, you and Abigail."

He froze.

It was snowing outside.

He drew back, pointing. "Amy, look."

She turned and spotted the flakes falling from the sky beyond the blinking Christmas tree.

"Oh, Flynn. It's beautiful."

He stepped in front of her again, cupping her face with his hands once more. "Yes," he said. "You are."

She was crying again.

"Stay with me?" he asked.

"For now and always," she answered softly.

Epilogue

Please don't blow it. Please don't blow it. Please don't blow it.

"Ready the carriage," Amy said softly after pressing the button on her wireless mic.

"Roger that," said her assistant, Fiona, outside Maverick and Charlotte's house, her youthful enthusiasm evident in the gleeful tone of her voice. She was a high school student Amy hired during wedding season, and probably the only other person in the world who loved weddings as much as she did.

It had dawned a glorious day for the Gillian-Bennett wedding. As the day had faded into the gentle hues of dusk, the sky had turned a brilliant blue dotted by high clouds an eggshell pink. Amy sighed as she caught a glimpse of it through the sliding glass doors at the back of the house.

"Are you coming?" she called down the hall.

The bedroom door opened, Aunt Crystal standing

back to let Charlotte by, resplendent in a floor-length white gown that left her shoulders bare and hugged her waist.

"Ready," Jayden answered for them all—Ava, Jayden and Aunt Crystal, all of whom emerged behind Charlotte.

"You look amazing," Amy told Charlotte, eyeing her dress up and down, checking for spots and wrinkles or missing pearls…anything that might stand out in a photograph. Usually she knelt down and examined things up close, but there was no way she could squat anymore. Not with her stomach. Once so flat, it had taken on the dimensions of the Death Star. So she did a visual scan, and as she did, she suddenly realized her friends were strangely silent.

"What's going on?" she asked. Dear goodness, had something happened? What? Did someone forget their heels? But everyone looked splendid in their bridesmaid's dresses, including Jayden, who'd delivered her baby and so wore a floor-length gown in a shade of blue. They all wore shades of blue. Was it her, then? Did she have jelly on her belly? She glanced down at the pretty floral dress she wore just to be sure, but there were no stains.

"Why do you guys all look like you've swallowed frogs?" she asked.

"Shall we tell her?" Jayden asked Charlotte.

"Go ahead," Charlotte said.

"Well," Jayden said. "You don't happen to have any sparkling apple cider Charlotte could use in place of champagne today, do you?"

All the women stared at her expectantly, Charlotte's lips twitching, Crystal still appearing a little shell-shocked. Ava and Jayden clearly amused. It took Amy a second to glean their meaning. And then she stepped back in surprise, nearly colliding with a giant house-plant.

"No way," she gasped.

Charlotte nodded, and Amy realized she'd been crying earlier.

"Way," Jayden said.

"I just found out," Charlotte said, "like, ten seconds ago. Jayden forced me to take a pregnancy test just now."

"On her wedding day?" Amy asked.

"See," Crystal said, "I'm not the only one to consider that crazy."

"I wanted to know," said the bridesmaid.

"Oh, my goodness, Charlotte," Amy said with a shake of her head. "I would hug you except I don't think I can get close enough with this huge stomach of mine. Besides, I know if I do, I'll start crying, and then you'll start crying, and then your makeup will have to be redone and we don't have time for that." Amy gently clasped her pearl-and-lace-clad arm. "I'm just so tickled, though."

"Thank you," Charlotte said.

"You're going to be the most amazing mom," Amy added.

"She will be," said Jayden.

They all three looked ready to cry.

"No," Amy said, sucking in a breath. "You guys will not cry. I need you all out front. But someone needs to grab Olivia on their way." She clapped her hands. "Ava, make sure her dress doesn't snag on anything as she walks toward the front door. Jayden, dash ahead and open the door, will you? I'm going to help Aunt Crystal find her missing earring."

"My missing what?" Her hands shot to her ears, her eyes widening when she realized one was missing. "Oh, my goodness. Where did it go?"

"It's probably in the bedroom where you changed." She looked at the other three women. "Go," she barked, all business now, but she smiled. She couldn't help herself. Charlotte pregnant. How exciting.

They found Crystal's earring where she thought it would be, on the floor of the guest bedroom. She watched as Crystal slipped it back on, then checked her upswept hair and shimmering blue dress, nodding before marching her toward the front of the house. They all piled into the massive stagecoach that now belonged to the ranch, Olivia squealing and clapping in delight. Amy was so tickled with how it looked that she shivered in excitement. They'd used some kind of veterinary wrapping to hold the lights in place around the horses' legs. The weather couldn't be more perfect, too.

"Let's do this," she said into her mic.

Fiona headed toward Old Greenie, which sat in front of the carriage. Amy waved goodbye to the ladies inside, then slipped into the driver's seat of the four-wheeled vehicle, and as she did, she couldn't help but recollect the first time she'd seen it, and how amazingly different her life was now. Flynn had become her best friend. Her confidant. Her biggest cheerleader, and she didn't know what she'd do without him.

"Let's roll," she said to her assistant, heading up the hill, the sound of horses' hooves erupting behind them.

She passed the stables, the roads all lined with cars, their guests already up at the meadow, but Amy remembered when Flynn had introduced her to his favorite broodmare and her baby. As she drove up the hill, she remembered how nervous she'd been to meet Flynn's entire family on Thanksgiving Day. They shot past Reese Gillian's house; Flynn's dad was already at Aunt Crystal's house, where the men of the family had gotten dressed.

"All right," she said to Fiona as they made the left toward Crystal and Bob's house. Yikes. It was a good thing she'd put out parking cones to block people from parking out front. The carriage would barely have room to squeeze by.

"Fiona, you make sure Maverick's in place." She put the brake on, hopped out and removed cones. "Let me know if there are any problems with the lights, too," she said once she returned to the vehicle, "although there shouldn't be. It looked great when I turned them on earlier, then again it was hard to tell because it was still daylight, but now it's dusk, so let me know."

"Will do," said Fiona.

Amy all but skidded to a stop in Aunt Crystal's driveway.

"I need to check in with the caterer," Amy said. "I swear I'm never using them again. They about gave me a heart attack when they weren't here on time."

"Amy," Fiona said, resting a hand on her arm. "Relax. Everything is going to be fine. It looks amazing."

Amy stared into the teenager's eyes. It did. To her right, the pathway sparkled with lights. Hundreds and hundreds of them all leading the way to the meadow and the massive tree and the lights around the perimeter and the benches Flynn's brother Carson had carved for the guests to sit on. The dozens and dozens of flowers she'd placed in old vases and tin tubs.

"I know it will be."

The carriage arrived. Olivia was the first out, clearly beyond excited and wanting to pet the horses pulling the stagecoach. All the others stepped out. The only fly in her ointment was how Flynn barely glanced at her while she rounded everyone up for a pre-walk-down-the-aisle chat. She reminded them of who was walking down the aisle with whom, and for one of them to remind Olivia of what to do when they arrived at the meadow, then checked to make sure they all looked perfect.

"Flowers," Amy suddenly said. "Where are the flowers?"

"Here," said Flynn, bringing over a box.

Thank you, she silently telegraphed, but he didn't even smile, and then Fiona radioed that everything looked good at the meadow. That was her cue to start the wedding party down the path. She dashed ahead of them, first, checking lights on her way. It all looked good. Better than good. When she made it to the clearing, she paused for a moment because it took her breath away, that tree. With the sun dipping behind the horizon, the tree looked like a living lightning bolt, dazzling in its splendor and so bright that the guests on the benches in front of it were in shadow. Later, the bride and groom would take off for their honeymoon in the lit coach, and she couldn't wait to see the guests' reactions to that. She'd never been more proud of her hard work in her life.

"Isn't it amazing?" Fiona asked softly.

"Yes, but we need to turn up the music. You can barely hear it." She turned to her helper. "Make sure Charlotte hangs down the path a bit. I'll give you a signal when it's time for her to walk down the aisle."

She didn't even wait for Fiona to answer, just raced as best she could over to a corner of the meadow where they'd set up a dance floor. They had tables all around the perimeter of the meadow, and she had to cross between them to get to where the music played. She tapped her right ear, the man clearly understanding her meaning because he bent toward the table he had set up behind the bales and suddenly the music got louder. It actually worked in their favor because the guests sitting on the benches stirred, turning toward the pathway. Once again, her eyes found Flynn, but he was watching Crystal lead Olivia down the aisle, the little girl dropping her petals. They peeled off two by two, the groomsmen and their bridesmaids. All too quickly, a hush settled over the crowd.

"We're ready for her," Amy whispered into her mic. She signaled for the wedding march music to play. The guests stood, and this was it: the moment Amy loved the most. The sighs from the crowd. The look of joy on Charlotte's face. The loving glance she exchanged with her groom. It was Amy's favorite part of the day.

It went flawlessly from there on out, too. There was laughter when Charlotte and Maverick said their vows. Tears, too. At one point, Sadie, Maverick and Charlotte's dog, barked, but no one seemed to notice. Her heart swelled when, at the end, they announced the bride and groom, and the guests stood up and clapped.

Done.

Well, that part at least. Time to check the tables. Make sure the caterers hadn't forgotten any of the food. Double-check the wedding cake was okay. The list was endless.

"You did a good job," someone said.

She turned. It was Flynn, and she was so glad to see him she instantly sank into his arms.

"Whoa," he laughed because she nearly knocked him off his feet.

"I'm sorry," she said. It felt good—so, so good—to absorb his warmth and strength. He must have been nervous earlier. That must have been why he'd barely spared her a glance.

"Don't be sorry," he said. "You must be exhausted."

She leaned back. "I am, but it's been worth it."

He was staring down at her strangely and suddenly she realized the crowd around her had gone quiet. She looked past Flynn, spotted Crystal behind him. To her left stood Jayden, the bride and groom on her right.

"What's going on?"

A crowd began to form around them and Amy's heart began to pound because Flynn was reaching into his pocket and sinking down to one knee and she gasped, even took a step back.

"Amy," he said, looking up at her. "I couldn't think of a better day to ask you this question. A day when everyone's hearts are filled with joy for Charlotte and Maverick. When we're surrounded by so many friends and family. Of course, I had to ask the bride and groom if they would mind me stealing some of their thunder, but they were only too happy to agree."

She glanced at Charlotte and Maverick and their smiles were so full of love that Amy wanted to cry.

Flynn opened a box. A diamond ring sat inside, the stone catching the lights she'd strewed around the meadow, sparkling. Her hands flew to her cheeks because it felt like a dream.

"Will you marry me, Amy?"

She closed her eyes, replaying the words in her mind, and her heart.

Will you marry me?

He wanted her. Wanted Abigail, too. It didn't matter that she was pregnant or that she had this crazy life creating these crazy weddings. He loved her, so much so that he'd arranged this whole thing in front of family and friends.

"Yes," she all but whispered. "Yes. Of course."

The crowd erupted. Flynn stood, beaming, as he slipped a ring on her finger.

"Finally," someone said. Jayden, Amy thought.

Flynn pulled her into his arms again, and Amy started to cry, but this time, for a completely different reason than all the times before. This time she cried out of joy and, yes, in disbelief, because no matter what she told herself, there would always be a tiny part of her that wondered if she was worthy of this family's love.

He pulled back, smiling down at her tenderly. "Surprise," he said.

And it was then, as she looked into his eyes, that she finally let go of her insecurities. How could she be anything but strong and courageous and a good mommy with Flynn by her side?

"I love you, Flynn," she whispered.

"I love you, too," he whispered back.

He bent, kissing her softly, and Amy realized today wasn't just the start of Maverick and Charlotte's life, it was the start of hers, too. And that life would be amazing and wonderful and full of surprises.

And it was.

* * * * *

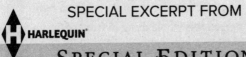

SPECIAL EXCERPT FROM

HARLEQUIN

SPECIAL EDITION

> *Alyssa Santangelo has no memory of the*
> *past seven years—including her divorce—but she*
> *remembers her love for Connor Bravo. One way*
> *or another, she's going to get her husband back.*

> *Read on for a sneak preview of*
> A Husband She Couldn't Forget,
> *the next book in Christine Rimmer's*
> *The Bravos of Valentine Bay miniseries.*

An accident. I've been in an accident. The stitches they'd
put in her knee throbbed dully, her cheeks and forehead
burned and she had a mild headache. Every time she took
a breath, she remembered that the seat belt had not been
very nice to her.

She must have made a noise, because as she sagged
back to the pillow again, Dante flinched and opened
his eyes. "Hey, little sis." He'd always called her that,
even though she was second eldest, after him. "How you
feelin'?"

"Everything aches," she grumbled. "But I'll live."
Longing flooded her for the comfort of her husband's
strong arms. She needed him near. He would soothe all
her pains and ease her weird, formless fears. "Where's
Connor gotten off to?"

Dante's mouth fell half-open, as though in bafflement at her question. "Connor?"

He looked so befuddled, she couldn't help chuckling a little, even though laughing made her chest and ribs hurt. "Yeah. Connor. You know, that guy I married nine years ago—my husband, your brother-in-law?"

Dante sat up. He also continued to gape at her like she was a few screwdrivers short of a full tool kit. "Uh, what's going on? You think you're funny?"

"Funny? Because I want my husband?" She bounced back up to a sitting position. "What exactly is happening here? I mean it, Dante. Be straight with me. Where's Connor?"

Don't miss
A Husband She Couldn't Forget
by Christine Rimmer,
available October 2019 wherever
Harlequin® Special Edition books and ebooks are sold.

www.Harlequin.com

Looking for more satisfying love stories
with community and family at their core?

Check out **Harlequin® Special Edition**
and **Love Inspired®** books!

New books available every month!

CONNECT WITH US AT:

Facebook.com/groups/HarlequinConnection

 Facebook.com/HarlequinBooks

 Twitter.com/HarlequinBooks

 Instagram.com/HarlequinBooks

 Pinterest.com/HarlequinBooks

ReaderService.com

**ROMANCE WHEN
YOU NEED IT**

HFGENRE2018

Looking for inspiration in tales
of hope, faith and heartfelt romance?

Check out **Love Inspired**® and
Love Inspired® **Suspense** books!

New books available every month!

SPECIAL EXCERPT FROM

Love Inspired®

*Could a pretend Christmastime courtship
lead to a forever match?*

Read on for a sneak preview of
Her Amish Holiday Suitor, *part of Carrie Lighte's
Amish Country Courtships miniseries.*

Nick took his seat next to her and picked up the reins, but before moving onward, he said, "I don't understand it, Lucy. Why is my caring about you such an awful thing?" His voice was quivering and Lucy felt a pang of guilt. She knew she was overreacting. Rather, she was reacting to a heartache that had plagued her for years, not one Nick had caused that evening.

"I don't expect you to understand," she said, wiping her rough woolen mitten across her cheeks.

"But I want to. Can't you explain it to me?"

Nick's voice was so forlorn Lucy let her defenses drop. "I've always been treated like this, my entire life. *Lucy's too weak, too fragile, too small, she can't go outside or run around or have any fun because she'll get sick. She'll stop breathing. She'll wind up in the hospital.* My whole life, Nick. And then the one little taste of utter abandon I ever experienced—charging through the dark with a frosty wind whisking against my face, feeling totally invigorated and alive… You want to take that away from me, too."

She was crying so hard her words were barely intelligible, but Nick didn't interrupt or attempt to quiet her. When she finally settled down and could speak

LIEXP0919

normally again, she sniffed and asked, "May I use your handkerchief, please?"

"Sorry, I don't have one," Nick said. "But here, you can use my scarf. I don't mind."

The offer to use Nick's scarf to dry her eyes and blow her nose was so ridiculous and sweet all at once it caused Lucy to chuckle. "*Neh*, that's okay," she said, removing her mittens to dab her eyes with her bare fingers.

"I really am sorry," he repeated.

Lucy was embarrassed. "That's all right. I've stopped blubbering. I don't need a handkerchief after all."

"*Neh*, I mean I'm sorry I treated you in a way that made you feel…the way you feel. I didn't mean to. I was concerned. I care about you and I wouldn't want anything to happen to you. I especially wouldn't want to play a role in hurting you."

Lucy was overwhelmed by his words. No man had ever said anything like that to her before, even in friendship. "It's not your fault," she said. "And I do appreciate that you care. But I'm not as fragile as you think I am."

"Fragile? You? I don't think you're fragile at all, even if you are prone to pneumonia." Nick scoffed. "I think you're one of the most resilient women I've ever known."

Lucy was overwhelmed again. If this kept up, she was going to fall hard for Nick Burkholder. Maybe she already had.

Don't miss
Her Amish Holiday Suitor *by Carrie Lighte,*
available October 2019 wherever
Love Inspired® books and ebooks are sold.

www.LoveInspired.com

Love Harlequin romance?

DISCOVER.

Be the first to find out about promotions,
news and exclusive content!

Facebook.com/HarlequinBooks

Twitter.com/HarlequinBooks

Instagram.com/HarlequinBooks

Pinterest.com/HarlequinBooks

ReaderService.com

EXPLORE.

Sign up for the Harlequin e-newsletter and
download a free book from any series at
TryHarlequin.com.

CONNECT.

Join our Harlequin community to share
your thoughts and connect with other
romance readers!
Facebook.com/groups/HarlequinConnection

HARLEQUIN®

**ROMANCE WHEN
YOU NEED IT**

HSOCIAL2018